LAWRENCE BLOCK

THE BURGLAR WHO LIKED TO QUOTE KIPLING

Mystery Guild Gold Presents The Fifty Greatest Crime Writers of the Twentieth Century

Margery Allingham

Robert Barnard

Lawrence Block

James M. Cain

John Dickson Carr

Raymond Chandler

Agatha Christie

Mary Higgins Clark

Michael Connelly

Patricia Cornwell

Amanda Cross

Colin Dexter

Arthur Conan Doyle

Daphne DuMaurier

Dick Francis

Erle Stanley Gardner

Elizabeth George

Sue Grafton

Graham Greene

John Grisham

Dashiell Hammett

Carl Hiassen

Patricia Highsmith

Reginald Hill

Tony Hillerman

Chester Himes

P.D. James

John LeCarre

Elmore Leonard

John D. MacDonald

Ross Macdonald

Ngaio Marsh

Ed McBain

Marcia Muller

Sara Paretsky

Robert B. Parker

Ellis Peters

Elizabeth Peters

Ellery Queen

Ruth Rendell

Craig Rice

Mary Roberts Rinehart

Dorothy L. Sayers

Georges Simenon

Mickey Spillane

Rex Stout

Josephine Tey

Ross Thomas

Donald Westlake

Cornell Woolrich

LAWRENCE BLOCK

THE BURGLAR WHO LIKED TO QUOTE KIPLING

THE BURGLAR WHO LIKED TO QUOTE KIPLING
A Literary Express, Inc. Book
(a subsidiary of Doubleday Direct, Inc.)
Reprinted by special arrangement with:
Dutton Signet,
a member of Penguin Putnam Inc.
375 Hudson Street
New York, NY 10014

Previously published by Signet, an imprint of Dutton Signet.
Previously published in a Dutton edition.

If you would be interested in purchasing additional copies of this
book, please write to this address for information:
Mystery Guild Gold
1540 Broadway
New York, NY 10036

ISBN: 1-58165-094-9

Printed in the United States of America

For Cheryl Morrison

A SHORT BIOGRAPHY
OF LAWRENCE BLOCK

LAWRENCE BLOCK's first short story was published in 1958; since that time he has published more than 50 books of fiction and nonfiction. A four-time winner of the Edgar Award (for the short stories "By the Dawn's Early Light," 1985; "Answers to Soldier," 1991; and "Keller's Therapy," 1994; and the novel *A Dance at the Slaughterhouse*, 1992), he has also won four Shamus Awards (*Eight Million Ways to Die*, 1983; "By the Dawn's Early Light," 1985; "The Merciful Angel of Death," 1994; *The Devil Knows You're Dead*, 1994), and was the first recipient of the Nero Wolfe Award (*The Burglar Who Liked to Quote Kipling*, 1980). He has been named a Grand Master by the Mystery Writers of America (1994) and has received numerous international awards in France, Germany and Japan. His work has been translated into 17 languages.

Equally renowned for both his comic work and his darker novels, Block has contributed two of the most well-known characters in crime fiction: hard boiled detective Matt Scudder and larcenous bookseller Bernie Rhodenbarr. New York City's Bryant Park is home to park benches dedicated to both characters. After a hiatus of almost 20 years, *Tanner on Ice* (1998) is the latest addition to a third series, begun in 1966, featuring Evan Tanner, *agent provocateur*.

Block is a regular contributor to *Playboy* magazine, and his short stories have been compiled in three collections. A longtime columnist for *Writer's Digest* magazine, he conducted a series of seminars for writers, and is the author of several books on the business of writing. Several of his novels have been adapted for film. His most recent books are *Hit Man* and *Everybody Dies*, both from William Morrow. A new Bernie Rhodenbarr mystery is forthcoming from Dutton.

Lawrence Block was born in Buffalo, New York, and currently resides with his wife in New York City's Greenwich Village.

FOREWORD

BY

LAWRENCE BLOCK

IN THE SPRING of 1976 I was living in Hollywood, in an establishment called the Magic Hotel. It was named for, and loosely affiliated with, the Magic Castle, a club for magicians that was something of a local institution. The hotel itself consisted of spacious one-bedroom apartments, occupied in the main by New York actors with short-term work in Los Angeles. The place was clean and well-managed, the rent was remarkably reasonable and I was very lucky to be there.

Nothing else in my life was going all that well. Someone, probably H. L. Mencken, once suggested that the hand of God had taken hold of the country by the state of Maine and lifted, so that everything loose wound up in Southern California. That's more or less how I'd gotten there, in a rusted-out Ford wagon, taking nine months and change to make the trip from New York. I was, you must understand, in no particular hurry, since I didn't really believe things would be any better there than they'd been in New York.

I was going through a bad patch, the details of which need not concern us here. Suffice it to say that my life wasn't working very well, and my career had ground to a halt. I wrote a few books that no one wanted to publish, and when I tried to write more, I couldn't get very far.

Sixty pages into a novel, I'd be unable to think of a reason for any of the characters to go on with it.

Writing, unfortunately, was the only work I'd done for the past 15 years, and the only thing I was at all qualified for. So I couldn't figure out what to do, and reading the employment classifieds just filled me with despair. *Man wanted to sweep up after the horses.* Hmmm, that sounds like something I might be able to do. *Experience a must.* No, never mind. Forget it.

And then one day a little voice said, "Don't rule out crime."

Let me interrupt this with a question. Are you sure you want to read this? Not the book, you're going to love the book. But this introduction. Like, what's the point?

I mean, it's not as though this is a book you have to read for class, or for a Great Books discussion group. Like its author, it's still too young to be a venerable classic, something that might require an introduction to place it in its historical context, or somehow make it a little easier for you to make heads or tails out of it. The books I write aren't hard to read. If there's one thing they are, it's accessible. They need an introduction about as much as Bernie needs a key to the front door.

This particular volume, handsomely printed and bound, may well hold up long enough to be read by another generation of readers, and, if present trends continue, the youngsters might need a little help working out the intricacies of anything written in complete sentences. An introduction might indeed serve them, if somebody can be found to explain it to them. But what has that got to do with you, Gentle Reader, living happily in the here and now?

You can read this book without assistance. As a matter of fact, there's a fair chance you've already read it. Perhaps you've bought this splendid edition because you wanted to upgrade from that ratty paperback copy before it falls apart altogether. Perhaps you once owned the book but made the common mistake of lending it out. You knew your friend would like it, and the scoundrel proved you right by liking it too much to return it. Well, you've replaced it at last, and you won't make the mistake of lending *this* copy, will you?

Are you beginning to get the point? Why are you wasting your time on this twaddle when you could be reading the book? Ready to fast forward? No?

Oh, all right. Let's get on with it, then . . .

ひ๑ひ

"Don't rule out crime," the voice said.

Ridiculous, I thought. Commit a crime and the world is made of glass, and a person could cut himself. What did I know about committing crimes?

"Experience is not a requirement," the voice countered. "Show somebody a gun, he doesn't ask to see your résumé."

Suppose I got arrested?

"It might be unpleasant," the voice allowed. "On the other hand, matters like food and clothing and shelter would no longer be a problem."

Hmmm, I thought.

But what kind of a criminal might I be? I at once ruled out anything that might put me on the receiving or inflicting end of violence. In fact, I would have to avoid any sort of confrontation. Embezzlement was not without appeal, but you had to have a job first.

Burglary, I thought, and the more I thought, the more I liked it. It seemed somehow akin to writing—you set your own hours, you avoided human contact and, if you were successful, you managed to touch the lives of people you never even met.

I began practicing, teaching myself to slip the lock of my hotel room with a credit card, which, alas, had long since ceased to have any other practical application. This proved handy one evening when I forgot my key, or would have, but for my having forgotten my credit card as well. I picked up a spare key at the desk and went to bed.

How far might I have gone with this? Hard to say. One afternoon, thinking about it, I wondered what I would do if the cops walked in on me in the middle of a burglary. I decided that, with a hitherto unblemished record, I'd probably get probation and return to the straight and narrow. And suppose, my writer's mind suggested, just suppose I surrendered, ready to cop a plea, and the police found a dead body in the next room. Then what?

That would be a problem, I thought.

A problem? Hell, that would be a *book*.

And over the next several weeks I wrote the opening chapters of *Burglars Can't be Choosers*.

I didn't intend for it to come out funny. Remember, I got the idea by imagining myself in the very fix Bernie finds himself in as the book opens, arrested for burglary with a murder victim in the next room. If there was anything intrinsically amusing in the situation, I couldn't see it.

But Bernie emerged, attitude in place, as I wrote the opening pages. This is coming out funny, I thought, more than a little perturbed. Instead of trying to fix it, I let it be what it wanted to be.

And Bernie saved me from a life of crime. Lee Wright at Random House read the opening chapters and struck a deal with my agent, and I finished the book and decided it was better than stealing.

I never expected I would write more than that single book about my buttoned-down burglar. But in the months following the first book's completion, I found him very much on my mind. I had enjoyed being that character during the writing of the book, seeing the world through his eyes, speaking in his distinctive voice. I had set the book in New York—even from 3,000 miles away it never occurred to me to set it anywhere else—and now I was living in New York once more, and I'd just finished slogging away to little purpose at a World War II novel, and why not write something I'd enjoy?

Random House published *The Burglar in the Closet*, and I seemed to be writing a series.

Well, almost. The way I see it, the *Burglar* books really became a series with the book you'll be able to read in a moment, as soon as we get this tedious introduction out of the way. *The Burglar Who Liked to Quote Kipling*—with this book, Bernie truly realized himself as a series character.

ৼৡৄৼ

Let me explain that. The character never really changed. I somehow knew who Bernie was from the moment he stepped on stage in the first book. But it was in *Kipling* that he got himself a life.

In the preceding books he has a few aspects of a life. He has an apartment, he has some friends and neighbors, he has a dentist, he has a friendly enemy in the person of Ray Kirschmann. But in the third book of the series he acquires the shop, Barnegat Books, and becomes not merely a burglar but an antiquarian bookseller as well. And, two doors down the street, he finds a best friend in the small person of Carolyn Kaiser, lesbian poodle-groomer. (The phrase, I should point out, can be confusing. Carolyn is a lesbian who grooms poodles, not a groomer of lesbian poodles.)

In *The Burglar Who Liked to Quote Kipling*, Bernie's world is fully realized. Other supporting players will turn up from time to time, and the action moves all over New York's five boroughs—and even makes a brief foray out of the city in *The Burglar in the Library*. But the basic dynamic never has to change.

The book received the first-ever Nero Wolfe Award, citing it as the best mystery of the year. I don't know that it's stronger or weaker than other books in the series, but I've always been pleased that it was the one to win the award, because of the way it set things up for the books that followed. If the *Burglar* books were a TV series, *Kipling* would be the pilot.

Five books in, Bernie went into a sort of suspended animation. *The Burglar Who Painted Like Mondrian* was well-received, and I certainly wanted to write more books about Bernie, but it began to look as though it wasn't going to happen. I made some brief attempts that aborted after 20 or 30 pages, and time passed, and Book #6 began to seem less and less likely.

But I kept thinking about Bernie and Carolyn. And, after an 11-year gap, I went off to San Francisco, holed up in a Tenderloin hotel, and wrote *The Burglar Who Traded Ted Williams.* And the books have come along every year or so ever since.

During the drought, I got the same question every time I made a public appearance. *When are you gonna write another book about Bernie?* Or, *Are you ever gonna write another book about Bernie?*

Finally, in a bookshop in Scottsdale, Arizona, I was able to answer that question as I'd longed to answer it. A sixth *Burglar* book was written, I informed the two nice ladies who'd inquired so plaintively. Moreover, it was scheduled for publication, and would be out in a matter of months.

They couldn't have been happier, and did everything but dance. Then their faces fell. Would this jubilation hurt the feelings of Matthew Scudder, my other series character? Might he take it amiss that they were making such a fuss over Bernie Rhodenbarr?

"Please," they begged, "don't misunderstand. We absolutely love Matt. But we want to marry Bernie."

Lawrence Block
Greenwich Village

When from 'ouse to 'ouse you're 'untin' you
          must always work in pairs—
    It 'alves the gain, but safer you will find—
For a single man gets bottled on them twisty-
          wisty stairs.
    An' a woman comes and clobs 'im from be'ind.
When you've turned 'em inside out, an' it seems
          beyond a doubt
    As if there weren't enough to dust a flute
          (*Cornet:* Toot! toot!)—
Before you sling your 'ook, at the 'ouse-tops take a
          look,
    For it's underneath the tiles they 'ide the loot.
          (*Chorus.*) 'Ow the loot!
              Bloomin' loot!
          That's the thing to make the boys git up
              an' shoot!
          It's the same with dogs an' men,
              If you'd make 'em come again
          Clap 'em forward with a Loo! loo! Lulu!
              Loot!
          Whoopee! Tear 'im, puppy! Loo! loo!
              Lulu!
          Loot! loot! Loot!

                              —Rudyard Kipling

                      "Loot"

ONE

I suppose he must have been in his early twenties. It was hard to be sure of his age because there was so little of his face available for study. His red-brown beard began just below his eyes, which in turn lurked behind thick-lensed horn-rims. He wore a khaki army shirt, unbuttoned, and beneath it his T-shirt advertised the year's fashionable beer, a South Dakota brand reputedly brewed with organic water. His pants were brown corduroy, his running shoes blue with a gold stripe. He was toting a Braniff Airlines flight bag in one ill-manicured hand and the Everyman's Library edition of *The Poems of William Cowper* in the other.

He set the book down next to the cash register, reached into a pocket, found two quarters, and placed them on the counter alongside the book.

"Ah, poor Cowper," I said, picking up the book. Its binding was shaky, which was why it had found its way to my bargain table. "My favorite's 'The Retired Cat.' I'm pretty sure it's in this edition." He shifted his weight from foot to foot while I scanned the table of contents. "Here it is. Page one-fifty. You know the poem?"

"I don't think so."

"You'll love it. The bargain books are forty cents or three for a dollar, which is even more of a bargain. You just want the one?"

"That's right." He pushed the two quarters an inch or so closer to me. "Just the one."

"Fine," I said. I looked at his face. All I could really see was his brow, and it looked untroubled, and I would have to do something about that. "Forty cents for the Cowper, and three cents for the Governor in Albany, mustn't forget him, and what does that come to?" I leaned over the counter and dazzled him with my pearly-whites. "I make it thirty-two dollars and seventy cents," I said.

"Huh?"

"That copy of Byron. Full morocco, marbled end-papers, and I believe it's marked fifteen dollars. The Wallace Stevens is a first edition and it's a bargain at twelve. The novel you took was only three dollars or so, and I suppose you just wanted to read it because you couldn't get anything much reselling it."

"I don't know what you're talking about."

I moved out from behind the counter, positioning myself between him and the door. He didn't look as though he intended to spring but he was wearing running shoes and you never can tell. Thieves are an unpredictable lot.

"In the flight bag," I said. "I assume you'll want to pay for what you took."

"This?" He looked down at the flight bag as if astonished to find it dangling from his fingers. "This is just my gym stuff. You know—sweat socks, a towel, like that."

"Suppose you open it."

Perspiration was beading on his forehead but he was trying to tough it out. "You can't make me," he said. "You've got no authority."

"I can call a policeman. He can't make you open it,

either, but he can walk you over to the station house and book you, and *then* he can open it, and do you really want that to happen? Open the bag."

He opened the bag. It contained sweat socks, a towel, a pair of lemon-yellow gym shorts, and the three books I had mentioned along with a nice clean first edition of Steinbeck's *The Wayward Bus,* complete with dust wrapper. It was marked $17.50, which seemed a teensy bit high. "I didn't get that here," he said.

"You have a bill of sale for it?"

"No, but—"

I scribbled briefly, then gave him another smile. "Let's call it fifty dollars even," I said, "and let's have it."

"You're charging me for the Steinbeck?"

"Uh-huh."

"But I had it with me when I came in."

"Fifty dollars," I said.

"Look, I don't want to *buy* these books." He rolled his eyes at the ceiling. "Oh God, why did I have to come in here in the first place? Look, I don't want any trouble."

"Neither do I."

"And the last thing I want is to buy anything. Look, keep the books, keep the Steinbeck too, the hell with it. Just let me get out of here, huh?"

"I think you should buy the books."

"I don't have the money. I got fifty cents. Look, keep the fifty cents too, okay? Keep the shorts and the towel, keep the sweat socks, okay? Just let me get the hell out of here, okay?"

"You don't have any money?"

"No, nothing. Just the fifty cents. Look—"

"Let's see your wallet."

"What are you— I don't have a wallet."

"Right hip pocket. Take it out and hand it to me."

"I don't believe this is happening."

I snapped my fingers. "The wallet."

It was a nice enough black pinseal billfold, complete with the telltale outline of a rolled condom to recall my own lost adolescence. There was almost a hundred dollars in the currency compartment. I counted out fifty dollars in fives and tens, replaced the rest, and returned the wallet to its owner.

"That's my money," he said.

"You just bought books with it," I told him. "Want a receipt?"

"I don't even want the books, dammit." His eyes were watering behind the thick glasses. "What am I going to do with them, anyway?"

"I suppose reading them is out. What did you plan to do with them originally?"

He stared at his track shoes. "I was going to sell them."

"To whom?"

"I don't know. Some store."

"How much were you going to get for them?"

"I don't know. Fifteen, twenty dollars."

"You'd wind up taking ten."

"I suppose so."

"Fine," I said. I peeled off one of his tens and pressed it into his palm. "Sell them to me."

"Huh?"

"Saves running from store to store. I can use good books, they're the very sort of item I stock, so why not take the ten dollars from me?"

"This is crazy," he said.

"Do you want the books or the money? It's up to you."

"I don't want the books."

"Do you want the money?"

"I guess so."

I took the books from him and stacked them on the counter. "Then put it in your wallet," I said, "before you lose it."

"This is the craziest thing ever. You took fifty bucks from me for books I didn't want and now you're giving me ten back. I'm out forty dollars, for God's sake."

"Well, you bought high and sold low. Most people try to work it the other way around."

"*I* should call a cop. I'm the one getting robbed."

I packed his gym gear into the Braniff bag, zipped it shut, handed it to him. Then I extended a forefinger and chucked him under his hairy chin.

"A tip," I said.

"Huh?"

"Get out of the business."

He looked at me.

"Find another line of work. Quit lifting things. You're not terribly good at it and I'm afraid you're temperamentally unsuited to the life that goes with it. Are you in college?"

"I dropped out."

"Why?"

"It wasn't relevant."

"Few things are, but why don't you see if you can't get back in? Pick up a diploma and find some sort of career that suits you. You're not cut out to be a professional thief."

"A professional—" He rolled his eyes again. "Jesus, I

ripped off a couple of books. Don't make a life's work out of it, huh?"

"Anybody who steals things for resale is a professional criminal," I told him. "You just weren't doing it in a very professional manner, that's all. But I'm serious about this. Get out of the business." I laid a hand lightly on his wrist. "Don't take this the wrong way," I said, "but the thing is you're too dumb to steal."

TWO

AFTER HE'D LEFT I tucked his forty dollars into my wallet, where it promptly became *my* forty dollars. I marked the Steinbeck down to fifteen dollars before shelving it and its companions. While doing this I spotted a few errant volumes and put them back where they belonged.

Browsers came and went. I made a few sales from the bargain table, then moved a Heritage Club edition of Virgil's *Eclogues* (boxed, the box water-damaged, slight rubbing on spine, price $8.50). The woman who bought the Virgil was a little shopworn herself, with a blocky figure and a lot of curly orange hair. I'd seen her before but this was the first time she'd bought anything, so things were looking up.

I watched her carry Virgil home, then settled in behind the counter with a Grosset & Dunlap reprint of *Soldiers Three*. I'd been working my way through my limited stock of Kipling lately. Some of the books were ones I'd read years ago, but I was reading *Soldiers Three* for the first time and really enjoying my acquaintance with Ortheris and Learoyd and Mulvaney when the little bells above my door tinkled to announce a visitor.

I looked up to see a man in a blue uniform lumbering across the floor toward me. He had a broad, open, honest face, but in my new trade one learned quickly not to judge a book by its cover. My visitor was Ray Kirschmann, the best cop money could buy, and money could buy him seven days a week.

"Hey, Bern," he said, and propped an elbow on the counter. "Read any good books lately?"

"Hello, Ray."

"Watcha readin'?" I showed him. "Garbage," he said. "A whole store full of books, you oughta read somethin' decent."

"What's decent?"

"Oh, Joseph Wambaugh, Ed McBain. Somebody who tells it straight."

"I'll keep it in mind."

"How's business?"

"Not too bad, Ray."

"You just sit here, buy books, sell books, and you make a livin'. Right?"

"It's the American way."

"Uh-huh. Quite a switch for you, isn't it?"

"Well, I like working days, Ray."

"A whole career change, I mean. Burglar to book-seller. You know what that sounds like? A title. You could write a book about it. *From Burglar to Bookseller.* Mind a question, Bernie?"

And what if I did? "No," I said.

"What the hell do you know about books?"

"Well, I was always a big reader."

"In the jug, you mean."

"Even on the outside, all the way back to childhood. You know what Emily Dickinson said. 'There is no frigate like a book.' "

"Frig it is right. You didn't just run around buyin' books and then open up a store."

"The store was already here. I was a customer over

the years, and I knew the owner and he wanted to sell out and go to Florida."

"And right now he's soakin' up the rays."

"As a matter of fact, I heard he opened up another store in St. Petersburg. Couldn't take the inactivity."

"Well, good for him. How'd you happen to come up with the scratch to buy this place, Bernie?"

"I came into a few dollars."

"Uh-huh. A relative died, somethin' like that."

"Something like that."

"Right. What I figure, you dropped out of sight for a month or so during the winter. January, wasn't it?"

"And part of February."

"I figure you were down in Florida doin' what you do best, and you hit it pretty good and walked with a short ton of jewelry. I figure you wound up with a big piece of change and decided Mrs. Rhodenbarr's boy Bernard oughta fix hisself up with a decent front."

"That's what you figure, Ray?"

"Uh-huh."

I thought for a minute. "It wasn't Florida," I said.

"Nassau, then. St. Thomas. What the hell."

"Actually, it was California. Orange County."

"Same difference."

"And it wasn't jewels. It was a coin collection."

"You always went for them things."

"Well, they're a terrific investment."

"Not with you on the loose they aren't. You made out like a bandit on the coins, huh?"

"Let's say I came out ahead."

"And bought this place."

"That's right. Mr. Litzauer didn't want a fortune for it. He set a fair price for the inventory and threw in the fixtures and the good will."

"Barnegat Books. Where'd you get the name?"

"I kept it. I didn't want to have to spring for a new sign. Litzauer had a summer place at Barnegat Light on the Jersey shore. There's a lighthouse on the sign."

"I didn't notice. You could call it Burglar Books. 'These books are a steal'—there's your slogan. Get it?"

"I'm sure I will sooner or later."

"Hey, are you gettin' steamed? I didn't mean nothin' by it. It's a nice front, Bern. It really is."

"It's not a front. It's what I do."

"Huh?"

"It's what I do for a living, Ray, and it's *all* I do for a living. I'm in the book business."

"Sure you are."

"I'm serious about this."

"Serious. Right."

"I am."

"Uh-huh. Listen, the reason I dropped in, I was thinkin' about you just the other day. What it was, my wife was gettin' on my back. You ever been married?"

"No."

"You're so busy gettin' settled, maybe marriage is the next step. Nothin' like it for settlin' a man. What she wanted, here it's October already and she's expectin' a long winter. You never met my wife, did you?"

"I talked to her on the phone once."

"The leaves are turnin' early, Ray. That means a cold winter.' That's what she tells me. If the trees don't turn until late, then *that* means a cold winter."

"She likes it cold?"

"What she likes is if it's cold and she's warm. What she's drivin' at is a fur coat."

"Oh."

"She goes about five-six, wears a size-sixteen dress.

Sometimes she diets down to a twelve, sometimes she packs in the pasta and gets up to an eighteen. Fur coats, I don't figure they got to fit like gloves anyway, right?"

"I don't know much about them."

"What she wants is mink. No wild furs or endangered species because she's a fanatic on the subject. Minks, see, they grow the little bastards on these ranches, so there's none of that sufferin' in traps, and the animal's not endangered or any of that stuff. All that they do is they gas 'em and skin 'em out."

"How nice for the minks. It must be like going to the dentist."

"Far as the color, I'd say she's not gonna be too fussy. Just so it's one of your up-to-date colors. Your platinum, your champagne. Not the old dark-brown shades."

I nodded, conjuring up an image of Mrs. Kirschmann draped in fur. I didn't know what she looked like, so I allowed myself to picture a sort of stout Edith Bunker.

"Oh," I said suddenly. "There's a reason you're telling me this."

"Well, I was thinkin', Bern."

"I'm out of the business, Ray."

"What I was thinkin', you might run into a coat in the course of things, know what I mean? I was thinkin' that you and me, we go back a ways, we been through a lot, the two of us, and—"

"I'm not a burglar anymore, Ray."

"I wasn't countin' on a freebie, Bernie. Just a bargain."

"I don't steal anymore, Ray."

"I hear you talkin', Bern."

"I'm not as young as I used to be. Nobody ever is but these days I'm starting to feel it. When you're young nothing scares you. When you get older everything does.

I don't ever want to go inside again, Ray. I don't like prisons."

"These days they're country clubs."

"Then they changed a whole hell of a lot in the past few years, because I swear I never cared for them myself. You meet a better class of people on the D train."

"Guy like you, you could get a nice job in the prison library."

"They still lock you in at night."

"So you're straight, right?"

"That's right."

"I been here how long? All that time you haven't had a single person walk in the store."

"Maybe the uniform keeps 'em away, Ray."

"Maybe business ain't what it might be. You been in the business how long, Bern? Six months?"

"Closer to seven."

"Bet you don't even make the rent."

"I do all right." I marked my place in *Soldiers Three*, closed the book, put it on the shelf behind the counter. "I made a forty-dollar profit from one customer earlier this afternoon and I swear it was easier than stealing."

"Is that a fact. You're a guy made twenty grand in an hour and a half when things fell right."

"And went to jail when they didn't."

"Forty bucks. I can see where that'd really have you turning handsprings."

"There's a difference between honest money and the other kind."

"Yeah, and the difference comes to somethin' like $19,960. This here, Bern, this is nickels and dimes. Let's be honest. You can't live on this."

"I never stole that much, Ray. I never lived that high. I got a small apartment on the Upper West Side, I stay out of night clubs, I do my own wash in the machines in the basement. The store's steady. You want to give me a hand with this?"

He helped me drag the bargain table in from the sidewalk. He said, "Look at this. A cop and a burglar both doin' physical work. Somebody should take a picture. What do you get for these? Forty cents, three for a buck? And that's keepin' you in shirts and socks, huh?"

"I'm a careful shopper."

"Look, Bern, if there's some reason you don't wanna help me out on this coat thing—"

"Cops," I said.

"What about cops?"

"A guy rehabilitates himself and you refuse to believe it. You talk yourselves hoarse telling me to go straight—"

"When the hell did I ever tell you to go straight? You're a first-class burglar. Why would I tell you to change?"

He let go of it while I filled a shopping bag with hardcover mysteries and began shutting down for the night. He told me about his partner, a clean-cut and soft-spoken young fellow with a fondness for horses and a wee amphetamine habit.

"All he does is lose and bitch about it," Ray complained, "until this past week when he starts pickin' the ponies with x-ray vision. Now all he does is win, and I swear I liked him better when he was losin'."

"His luck can't last forever, Ray."

"That's what I been tellin' myself. What's that, steel gates across the windows? You don't take chances, do you?"

I drew the gates shut, locked them. "Well, they were

already here," I said stiffly. "Seems silly not to use
them."

"No sense makin' it easy for another burglar, huh?
No honor among thieves, isn't that what they say? What
happens if you forget the key, huh, Bern?"

He didn't get an answer, nor do I suppose he expected
one. He chuckled instead and laid a heavy hand on my
shoulder. "I guess you'd just call a locksmith," he said.
"You couldn't pick the lock, not bein' a burglar anymore.
All you are is a guy who sells books."

❧❧❧

Barnegat Books is on East Eleventh Street between
Broadway and University Place. When I'd finished locking up I carried my shopping bag two doors east to a dog-
grooming salon called the Poodle Factory. Carolyn Kaiser had a skittish Yorkie up on the grooming table and
was buffing its little nails. She said, "Hey, is it that time
already? Just let me finish with Prince Philip here and
I'll be ready to go. If I don't get a drink in me soon I'll
start yipping like a chihuahua."

I got comfortable on the pillow sofa while Carolyn
put the final touches on the terrier's pedicure and
popped him back in his cage. During the course of this
she complained at length about her lover's misbehavior.
Randy had come home late the previous night, drunk
and disheveled and marginally disorderly, and Carolyn
was sick of it.

"I think it's time to end the relationship," she told
me, "but the question is how do I *feel* about ending the
relationship? And the answer is I don't *know* how I feel
because I can't get in *touch* with my feelings, and I figure
if I can't get in touch with them I might as well not feel

them altogether, so let's go someplace with a liquor license, because all I want to feel right now is better. And how was *your* day, Bernie?"

"A little long."

"Yeah, you do look faintly tuckered. Let's go, huh? I'm so sick of the smell of this place. I feel like I'm wearing Wet Dog perfume."

We ducked around the corner to a rather tired saloon called the Bum Rap. The jukebox leaned toward country and western, and Barbara Mandrell was singing about adultery as we took stools at the long dark bar. Carolyn ordered a vodka martini on the rocks. I asked for club soda with lime and got a nod from the bartender and a puzzled stare from Carolyn.

"It's October," she said.

"So?"

"Lent's in the spring."

"Right."

"Doctor's orders or something? Giving the old liver a rest?"

"Just don't feel like a drink tonight."

"Fair enough. Well, here's to crime. Hey, did I just say something wrong?"

So that got me onto the subject of Ray Kirschmann and his mink-loving wife, and it became Carolyn's turn to make sympathetic noises. We've become good at playing that role for one another. She's crowding thirty, with Dutch-cut dark-brown hair and remarkably clear blue eyes. She stands five-one in high heels and never wears them, and she's built like a fire hydrant, which is dangerous in her line of work.

I met her around the time I took over the bookshop. I didn't know Randy as well because I didn't see as much of her; the Poodle Factory was a solo venture of Carolyn's. Randy's a stewardess, or was until she got grounded for biting a passenger. She's taller and thinner than Carolyn, and a year or two younger, and faintly flighty. Randy and I are friends, I suppose, but Carolyn and I are soulmates.

My soulmate clucked sympathetically. "Cops are a pain," she said. "Randy had an affair with a cop once. I ever tell you?"

"I don't think so."

"She had this phase she went through, three months or so of panic before she was ready to come out as a lesbian. I think it was some kind of denial mechanism. She slept with dozens of men. This one cop was impotent and she made fun of him and he held his gun to her head and she thought he was going to kill her. Which somebody ought to, and why the *hell* am I talking about her again, will you tell me that?"

"Beats me."

"You got anything on tonight? You still seeing the woman from the art gallery?"

"We decided to go our separate ways."

"What about the crazy poet?"

"We never really hit it off."

"Then why don't you come by for dinner? I got something sensational working in the slow cooker. I put it in this morning before I remembered how mad I was. It's this Flemish beef stew with beer and shallots and mushrooms and all kinds of good things. I got plenty of Amstel for us to wash it down with, plus some Perrier if you're serious about this temperance bit."

I sipped my club soda. "I wish I could," I said. "But not tonight."

"Something on?"

"Just that I'm beat. I'm going straight home, and the

most active thing I intend to do is say a quick prayer to St. John of God."

"Is he somebody I should know about?"

"He's the patron saint of booksellers."

"Yeah? Who's the patron saint of dog groomers?"

"Damned if I know."

"I hope we've got one. I've been bitten and scratched and peed on and I ought to have someplace to turn. As far as that goes, I wonder if there's a patron saint of lesbians. All those cloistered nuns, there damn well ought to be. Seriously, do you suppose there is?"

I shrugged. "I could probably find out. I only know about St. John of God because Mr. Litzauer had a framed picture of him in the back room of the shop. But there must be books with lists of the patron saints. I've probably got something in the store, as far as that goes."

"It must be great, having that shop. Like living in a library."

"Sort of."

"The Poodle Factory's like living in a kennel. You going? Hey, have a nice night, Bern."

"Thanks. And I'll check out St. Sappho tomorrow."

"If you get a chance. Hey, is there a patron saint of burglars?"

"I'll check that, too."

 જ⟋⟍ખ

I rode three different subway trains to Broadway and Eighty-sixth and walked a block to Murder Ink, where I sold my shopping bag full of books to Carol Brener. She got all my vintage mysteries; I could do better wholesaling them to her than waiting for somebody to pick them off my shelves.

She said, "Charlie Chan, Philo Vance—this is wonderful, Bernie. I've got want-list customers for all this stuff. Buy you a drink?"

For a change everybody wanted to buy me a drink. I told her I'd take a rain check, left her shop just in time to miss a bus on West End Avenue, and walked the sixteen blocks downtown to my apartment. It was a nice crisp fall afternoon and I figured I could use the walk. You don't get all that much fresh air and exercise in a bookstore.

There was mail in my box. I carried it upstairs and put it in the wastebasket. I was half-undressed when the phone rang. It was a woman I know who runs a day-care center in Chelsea, and the parent of one of her charges had just given her two tickets to the ballet, and wasn't that terrific? I agreed that it was but explained I couldn't make it. "I'm bushed," I said. "I've ordered myself to go to bed without supper. I was just about to take the phone off the hook when it rang."

"Well, drink some coffee instead. What's-his-name's dancing. You know, the Russian."

"They're all Russians. I'd fall asleep in the middle. Sorry."

She wished me pleasant dreams and broke the connection. I left the phone off the hook. I'd have enjoyed eating Carolyn's beef stew and I'd also have enjoyed watching the Russian hop around the stage, and I didn't want the phone to let me know what else I was missing. It made an eerie sound for a while, then fell into a sullen silence. I finished undressing and turned off the lights and got into bed, and I lay there on my back with my arms at my sides and my eyes closed, breathing slowly and rhythmically and letting my mind go here and there. I either dreamed or daydreamed, and I was in some sort of doze when the alarm went off at nine o'clock. I got up, took a quick shower and shave, put on some clean clothes, and made myself a nice cup of tea. At a quarter after nine I put the phone back on the hook. At precisely nine-twenty it rang.

I picked it up and said hello. My caller said, "There's been no change."

"Good."

"Things are as planned at your end?"

"Yes."

"Good," he said, and rang off. No names, no pack drill. I looked at the telephone receiver for a moment, then hung it up, then thought better of it and took it off the hook once again. It whined for a while, but by the time I was done with my tea it was quiet.

I finished dressing. I was wearing a three-piece navy pinstripe suit, a Wedgwood-blue shirt, a tie with narrow green and gold diagonal stripes on a navy field. My shoes combined black calfskin moccasin-toe uppers and thick crepe soles. Wearing them, I made no sound as I scurried around the apartment, gathering up one thing and another, making my final preparations.

While my shoes were silent, my stomach was rumbling a bit. I hadn't eaten anything since lunch some nine hours earlier. But I didn't want to eat, and I knew better than to drink anything.

Not now.

I checked, made sure I had everything. I went out into the hall, double-locked my own door, then rode the elevator past the lobby to the basement, letting myself out via the service entrance to avoid passing my doorman.

The air had an edge to it. It wasn't cold enough for mink, but it was certainly topcoat weather. I had mine over my arm, and I took a moment to put it on.

Was there a patron saint of burglars? If so, I didn't know his name. I murmured a quick prayer, addressed it to whom it might concern, and set off to resume my life of crime.

THREE

Halfway across the Queensboro Bridge, I happened to glance at the fuel gauge. The needle was all the way over to the left, way past the big E, and I had what suddenly looked like a mile of bridge stretching out in front of me. I could see myself running out of gas smack in the middle of the East River. Horns would blare all around me, and when horns blare, can cops be far behind? They'd be understanding at first, because motorists do get stranded all the time, but their sympathy would fade when they learned I was driving a stolen car. And why, they might wonder, had I stolen a car without checking the gas?

I was wondering much the same thing myself. I stayed in lane and let my foot rest easy on the accelerator, trying to remember what the ecology commercials were always telling me about ways to conserve gasoline. No fast starts, no jamming on the brakes, and don't spend too much time warming up on cold mornings. Sound advice, all of it, but I couldn't see how it applied, and I clutched the steering wheel and waited for the engine to cut out and the world to cave in.

Neither of these things happened. I found a Chevron station a block from the bridge and told the attendant to fill the tank. The car was a sprawling old Pontiac with an engine that never heard about fuel crises, and I sat there and watched it drink twenty-two gallons of high-test. I wondered what the tank's capacity might be.

Twenty gallons, I decided, figuring the pumps were crooked. It's a dog-eat-dog world out there.

The tab came to fifteen dollars and change. I gave the kid a twenty and he gave me a smile in return and pointed to a sign on a pillar between the two pumps. You had to have exact change or a credit card after 8 P.M. *Help us thwart crime*, the sign urged. I don't know that they were thwarting anything, but they were certainly taking the profit out of it.

I have a couple of credit cards. I've even opened doors with them, although it's not the cinch TV shows might lead you to believe. But I didn't want a record of my presence in Queens, nor did I want anyone copying down the Pontiac's license number. So I let the little snot keep the change, which got me a mean grin, and I drove east on Queens Boulevard mumbling to myself.

It wasn't the money. What really troubled me was that I'd been driving around unwittingly with an empty tank. The thing is, I don't steal cars very often. I don't even drive them all that frequently, and when I do go and rent one for a weekend in the country, the Olins people give it to me with the tank full. I can be halfway to Vermont before I even have to think about gasoline.

I wasn't going to Vermont tonight, just to Forest Hills, and I could have gone there easily enough on the E train. That's how I'd made the trip a few days earlier when I did some basic reconnaissance. But I hadn't felt like coming home by subway, preferring as I do to avoid public transportation when my arms are full of somebody else's belongings.

And when I found the Pontiac on Seventy-fourth Street, I'd figured it for a sign from on high. GM cars are the easiest for me to get into and the simplest to start, and this one had Jersey plates, so no one would be surprised if I drove it eccentrically. Finally, the owner was unlikely to report it stolen. He'd parked it next to a fire hydrant, so he'd have to assume the cops had towed it away.

Jesse Arkwright lived in Forest Hills Gardens. Now Forest Hills itself is a nice solid middle-class neighborhood set south of Flushing Meadows in the very center of the Borough of Queens. Three out of four houses there contain at least one woman who plays mah-jongg when she's not at a Weight Watchers meeting. But Forest Hills Gardens is an enclave within an enclave, a little pocket of *haute bourgeoise* respectability. Every house is three stories tall, with gables and a tile roof. All of the lawns are manicured, all of the shrubbery under tight discipline. A neighborhood association owns the very streets themselves, keeping them in good repair and restricting on-street parking to neighborhood residents.

Cars from underprivileged neighborhoods make frequent forays into the quiet streets of Forest Hills Gardens, their occupants darting out to knock down matrons and make off with alligator handbags. And private police cruisers patrol those same streets twenty-four hours a day to keep that sort of thing to a minimum. It's not Beverly Hills, say, where every pedestrian is perforce a suspicious character, but the security's pretty tight.

It's even tighter on Copperwood Crescent, an elegant semicircle where massive piles of stone and brick sprawl on spacious wooded lots. The residents of Copperwood Crescent include a shipping-line heir, two upper-echelon mafiosi, the owner of a chain of budget funeral parlors, and two to three dozen similarly well-heeled citizens.

One private cop car has as its sole responsibility the safe-guarding of Copperwood Crescent, along with four ad-joining and similarly exclusive streets—Ironwood Place, Silverwood Place, Pewterwood Place, and Chancery Drive.

If Forest Hills Gardens is the soft underbelly of Queens, Copperwood Crescent is the ruby in its navel.

I didn't have any trouble finding the ruby. On my earlier trip I'd walked all around the neighborhood armed with pocket atlas and clipboard—a man with a clipboard never looks out of place. I'd found Copperwood Crescent then and I found it now, barely slowing the Pontiac as I rolled past Jesse Arkwright's house, an enor-mous beamed Tudor number. On each of the three floors a light burned in a mullioned window.

At the end of Copperwood Crescent I took a sharp left into Bellnap Court, a quiet block-long cul-de-sac that was out of bounds for the Copperwood-Ironwood-Silverwood-Pewterwood-Chancery patrol car. I parked at the curb between a couple of sizable oaks and cut the engine, removing my jumper wire from the ignition.

You need a sticker to park on the street, but that's to keep commuters from cluttering the area during daylight hours. Nobody gets towed at night. I left the car there and walked back to Copperwood Crescent. If the patrol car was on the job, I didn't see it, nor did I notice anyone else walking about.

The same three lights were lit in the Arkwright house. Without hesitation I walked the length of the driveway at the right of the house. I shined my pencil-beam flashlight through a garage window. A gleaming Jaguar sedan crouched on one side of the garage. The other stall was quite empty.

Good.

I went to the side door. Below the bell on the door-jamb was an inch-square metal plate slotted for a key. A red light glowed within, indicating that the burglar alarm was set. If I were Mr. Arkwright, equipped with the proper key, I could insert it in the slot and turn off the alarm. If, on the other hand, I were to insert anything other than the proper key, sirens would commence to sound and some signal would go off in the nearest police station.

Fine.

I rang the doorbell. The car was gone and the alarm was set, but you just never know, and the burglar least likely to wind up in slam is the sort of chap who wears suspenders and a belt, just in case. I'd rung this bell before, when I'd come calling with my clipboard, asking meaningless questions in aid of a nonexistent sewer survey. As then, I listened to the four-note chime sound within the large old house. I pressed my ear to the heavy door and listened carefully, and when the chimes quit echoing I heard nothing at all. No footsteps, no sign of human life. I rang again, and again I heard nothing.

Good.

I walked around to the rear of the house again. For a moment I just stood there. It was pleasant enough, the air uncharacteristically clear and clean. The moon wasn't visible from where I stood but I could see a scattering of stars overhead. What really awed me was the silence. Queens Boulevard was only blocks away but I couldn't hear any of its traffic. I suppose the trees kept the noise at bay.

I felt hundreds of miles from New York. The Arkwright house belonged in a Gothic novel, brooding over windswept moors.

Myself, I had no time for brooding. I put on my rubber gloves—skintight, their palms cut out for comfort's sake—and went to have a look at the kitchen door.

Thank God for burglar alarms and pickproof locks and tight security systems. They all help discourage the amateurs even as they give the citizenry a nice sense of safety and well-being. Without them, everybody would stash all the good stuff in safe-deposit boxes. Beyond that, they help make burglary the challenging occupation I've always found it. If any splay-fingered oaf could do as well, what fun would it be?

The Arkwright home had a first-rate burglar alarm, Fischer Systems' model NCN-30. I could see for myself that it was wired to all the ground-floor doors and windows. It might or might not have been connected to higher windows—most people don't take the trouble—but I didn't want to walk up a wall to find out one way or the other. It was simpler to rewire the system.

There are a few ways to beat a burglar alarm. One brutally direct method calls for cutting the lines supplying power to the house. This does lack subtlety—all the lights go out, for openers—and it's counter-productive when you're dealing with a good system like the NCN-30, because they have fail-safe devices that trigger them under such circumstances. (This can have interesting ramifications during a power failure, incidentally.)

Ah, well. I used some wires of my own, splicing them neatly into the picture, wrapping their ends ever so neatly with electrical tape, and by the time I was done the alarm was working as well as it had ever worked, but for the fact that it no longer covered the kitchen door. A regiment of cavalry could parade through that door without NCN-30 kicking up a fuss. The whole operation was more than your average burglar could do, and isn't it lucky that I'm not your average burglar?

With the alarm *hors de combat*, I turned my attention to the thick oak door, an *hors* of another color. A skeleton key opened its original lock, but there were two others, a Segal and a Rabson. I held my little flashlight in one hand and my ring of picks and probes in the other and went to work, pausing now and again to press an ear against the thick wood. (It's like seashells; if you listen carefully you can hear the forest.) When the last tumbler tumbled I turned the knob and tugged and shoved and nothing happened.

There was a manual bolt on the inside. I ran the flashlight beam down the edge of the door until I located it, then made use of a handy little tool I'd fashioned from a hacksaw blade, slipping it between door and jamb and working it to and fro until the bolt parted. I tried the door again, and wouldn't you know there was a chain lock that stopped it when it was three inches ajar? I could have sawed through that as well, but why? It was easier to slip my hand inside and unscrew the chain lock from its moorings.

I pushed the door all the way open and made an illegal entry a crooked accountant would have been proud of. For a moment I just stood there, glowing radiant. Then I closed the door and locked the locks. I couldn't do anything about the bolt I'd sawed through, but I did take a moment to restore the chain bolt.

Then I set out to explore the house.

There's absolutely nothing like it.

Forget everything I said to Ray Kirschmann. True, I was getting older. True, I shrank from the prospect of getting chewed by attack dogs and shot by irate householders and locked by the authorities in some pick-proof penitentiary cell. True, true, all of it true, and so what? None of it mattered a whit when I was inside someone else's dwelling place with all his worldly goods spread out before me like food on a banquet table. By God, I wasn't *that* old! I wasn't *that* scared!

I'm not proud of this. I could spout a lot of bilge about the criminal being the true existential hero of our times, but what for? I don't buy it myself. I'm not nuts about criminals and one of the worst things about prison was having to associate with them. I'd prefer to live as an honest man among honest men, but I haven't yet found an honest pursuit that lets me feel this way. I wish there were a moral equivalent of larceny, but there isn't. I'm a born thief and I love it.

～⟨⟩～

I made my way through a butler's pantry and an enormous brick-floored kitchen, crossing a hallway to the formal living room. The light I'd noted from the street cast a warm glow over the room. It was a noteworthy object in and of itself, a leaded-glass dragonfly lamp by Tiffany. I'd last seen one in an antique shop on upper Madison Avenue with a $15,000 tag on it, and that was a few years ago.

But I hadn't come all the way to Queens to steal furniture. I'd come with a very specific purpose, and I didn't really need to be in the living room at all. I didn't have to

take inventory, but old habits die hard, and I could
hardly avoid it.

The lamp made it easy, saving me the trouble of using my flashlight. There was a timer so that it would
turn itself off during daylight hours and resume its vigil
at dusk, burning bravely until dawn, announcing to passers-by that nobody was home.

Considerate of them, I thought, to leave a light for
the burglar.

The lamp was perched on an ornamental French
kneehole desk. Four of the desk's six drawers were fakes,
but one of the others held a Patek Philippe pocket watch
with a hunting scene engraved on its case.

I closed the drawer without disturbing the watch.

The dining room was worth a look. A sideboard absolutely loaded with silver, including two complete sets of
sterling tableware and a ton of hallmarked Georgian
serving pieces. No end of fine porcelain and crystal.

I left everything undisturbed.

The library, also on the ground floor, was a room I
would have gladly called my own. It measured perhaps
twelve by twenty feet, with a glorious Kerman carpet
covering most of the buffed parquet floor. Custom-built
bookshelves of limed English oak lined two walls. In the
middle of the room, centered beneath a fruited Tiffany
shade, stood a tournament-size pool table. At the room's
far end, twin portraits of Arkwright ancestors in gilded
oval frames looked down in solemn approbation.

A pair of wall racks, one holding cue sticks, the other a locked cabinet that displayed sporting rifles and shotguns. A couple of overstuffed leather chairs. An elaborate bar, the crystal glassware etched with game birds in flight. Enough liquor in one form or another to float a fair-sized cabin cruiser, plus decanters of sherry and port and brandy placed at convenient intervals about the room. A smoker's stand, mahogany, with a few dozen briar pipes and two cased meerschaums. A cedar cabinet of Havanas. A whole room of brass and wood and leather, and I yearned to nail the door shut and pour myself a stiff Armagnac and stay there forever.

Instead I scanned the bookshelves. They were a jumble, but there was no shortage of dollar value. While they ran heavily to uncut sets of leather-bound memoirs of unremembered hangers-on at pre-Revolutionary Versailles, there were plenty of other items as well, many of which I'd never seen outside of the catalogs of the better book dealers and auction galleries. I happened on a pristine first of Smollet's rarest novel, *The Adventures of Sir Laurence Greaves*, and there were any number of fine bindings and important first editions and Limited Editions Club issues and private press productions, all arranged in no discernible order and according to no particular plan.

I took one book from the shelves. It was bound in green cloth and not much larger than an ordinary paperback. I opened it and read the flowing inscription on the flyleaf. I paged through it, closed it, and put it back on the shelf.

I left the library as I'd found it.

The stairs were dark. I used my flashlight, went up and down the staircase three times. There was one board that creaked and I made sure I knew which one it was. Fourth from the top.

The others were comfortingly silent.

Twin beds in the master bedroom, each with its own bedside table. His and hers closets. His ran to Brooks Brothers suits and cordovan shoes. I especially liked one navy suit with a muted stripe. It wasn't that different from the one I was wearing. Her closet was full of dresses and furs, including one Ray's wife would have salivated over. Good labels in everything. A drawer in the dressing table—French Provincial, white enamel, gold trim—held a lot of jewelry. A cocktail ring caught my eye, a stylish little item with a large marquise-cut ruby surrounded by seed pearls.

There was some cash in the top drawer of one of the bedside tables, a couple hundred dollars in tens and twenties. In the other table I found a bankbook—eighteen hundred dollars in a savings account in the name of Elfrida Grantham Arkwright.

I didn't take any of these things. I didn't take the Fabergé eggs from the top of the chest of drawers, or the platinum cuff links and tie bar, or any of the wrist-watches, or, indeed, anything at all.

In Jesse Arkwright's study, all the way at the rear of the house's second floor, I found a whole batch of bankbooks. Seven of them, secured by a rubber band, shared the upper right drawer of his desk with postage stamps and account ledgers and miscellaneous debris. The savings accounts all had sizable balances and the quick mental total I ran came to a little better than sixty thousand dollars.

I'll tell you. It gave me pause.

I once knew a fellow who'd been tossing an apartment in Murray Hill, filling a pillowcase with jewelry and silver, when he came across a bankbook with a balance in five figures. Clever lad that he was, he promptly turned his pillowcase inside out and put everything back where he'd found it. He left the premises looking as though he'd never visited them in the first place, taking nothing but that precious bankbook. That way the residents wouldn't know they'd been burgled, and wouldn't miss the bankbook, and he could drain their account before they suspected a thing.

Ah, the best-laid plans. He presented himself at the teller's window the very next morning, withdrawal slip in hand and bankbook at the ready. It was a small withdrawal—he was merely testing the waters—but that particular teller happened to know that particular depositor by sight, and the next thing the chap knew he was doing a medium-long bit in Dannemora, which is where I ran into him.

So much for bankbooks.

So much, too, for a double handful of Krugerrands, those large gold coins the South Africans stamp out for people who want to invest in the yellow metal. I like gold—what's not to like?—but they were in a drawer with a handgun, and I dislike guns at least as much as I like gold. The ones in the library were for show, at least. This one was here for shooting burglars.

So much for the Krugerrands. So much, too, for a

shoulder-height set of glassed-in shelves full of Boehm birds and Art Nouveau vases and glass paperweights. I spotted a Lalique ashtray just like the one on my grandmother's coffee table, and a positive gem of a Daum Nancy vase, and Baccarat and Millefiori weights galore, and—

It was starting to get to me. I couldn't look anywhere without seeing ten things I wanted to steal. Every flat surface in that study held bronzes, all of them impressive. Besides the usual bulls and lions and horses, I noticed one of a camel kneeling alongside a Legionnaire. The latter wore a kepi on his head and a pained expression on his face, as if he were sick of jokes about Legionnaire's Disease.

A couple of stamp albums. One general worldwide collection that didn't look to be worth much, but the other was a Scott Specialty Album for the Benelux countries, and a quick thumbing didn't reveal too many blank spaces.

And a coin collection. Lord above, a coin collection! No albums, just a dozen black cardboard boxes two inches square and ten inches long. Each was crammed to capacity with two-by-two coin envelopes. I didn't have time to check them but I couldn't resist. I opened one box at random and found it was filled with Barber quarters and halves, all Proofs or Uncirculated specimens. Another box contained superb Large Cents catalogued by Sheldon numbers.

How could I possibly leave them?

I left them. I didn't take a thing.

I was in one of the guest bedrooms on the second floor, playing my penlight over the walls and admiring a very nice pencil-signed Rouault lithograph, when I heard a car in the driveway. I checked my watch. It was 11:23. I listened as the automatic garage door swung upward, listened as the car's engine cut out. As the garage door swung down again I quit listening and walked the length of the hall to the staircase leading to the third floor. I was up those stairs and crouching on the third-floor landing by the time Jesse Arkwright's key hit the slot at the side of the house. First he turned off the burglar alarm, then he opened the door, and I fancied I could hear him refastening half a dozen locks after he and Elfrida had made their entrance.

Muffled conversation, barely audible two floors below me. I moved a rubber-gloved forefinger and wiped perspiration from my forehead. I'd planned on this, of course. I'd even checked the attic stairs earlier to make sure there were no squeakers in the lot.

All the same, I didn't like it. Burglary's a tightly wired proposition at best, but I generally get to do my work in precious solitude. If householders come home while I'm on the job, my usual impulse is to depart abruptly.

This time I had to linger.

Two floors below, a teakettle whistled briefly, then sighed as someone removed it from the flame. For an instant I'd mistaken its cry for a police siren. Nerves, I thought, taking deep breaths, beseeching the patron saint of burglars for a dose of serenity.

Maybe I'd been right when I talked to Kirschmann. Maybe I was getting too old for this. Maybe I didn't have the requisite sang-froid. Maybe—

Crouching was uncomfortable. I got stiffly to my feet.

The attic was finished off, its central hallway covered with a length of faded maroon carpeting. I walked clear to the front of the house, where a brass floorlamp equipped with a timer sent out forty watts' worth of light through a curtained window. A maid's room, it looked to be, although the household no longer employed live-in servants.

A day bed stretched along one wall. I lay down on top of it, pulled a green and gold afghan coverlet over myself, and closed my eyes.

I couldn't really hear much from where I was. At one point I thought I heard footsteps on the stairs, and then a few moments later I fancied that I could hear the clatter of balls on the pool table in the library. This was probably a case of my imagination filling in the blanks. After an evening at the theater, the Arkwright routine was supposed to be quite predictable. Home around eleven-thirty, a spot of coffee and something sweet in the breakfast nook, and then Elfrida would pop upstairs with a book of crosswords while Jesse ran a rack or two at the pool table, nipped at one of the crystal decanters, read a few pages of one of his leather-bound classics, and then hied his own bulk up the stairs and joined his wife in their chamber.

Would he take a final tour of the downstairs, making sure all the doors were locked? Would he happen to check the sliding bolt on the kitchen door, and would he happen to notice that some clever chap had sawn through it? Was he, even as I thought these grim thoughts, lifting a receiver to summon the local constabulary?

I could have been at the ballet, watching a Russian imitate a gazelle. I could have gone home with Carolyn and eaten Flemish stew and drunk Dutch beer. Or I could have been home in my own little bed.

I stayed where I was and waited.

꒜꒨꒜

At one-thirty I got to my feet. I hadn't heard a sound within the house for an entire half-hour. I padded silently to the stairs, crossing right over the master bedroom where I hoped my hosts were sleeping soundly. I went down the stairs, treading ever so gingerly on my crepe soles, and I crossed the second-floor hallway and went on down the other stairs to the ground floor. It was no great feat to remember to avoid the fourth step from the top; I'd obsessed on that very subject for the past twenty minutes.

The lights were out once again on the ground floor, except for the indomitable dragonfly lamp in the living room. I didn't have to use my penlight to find my way to the library, but once I was in that room I played its beam here and there.

Arkwright had paid the room his nightly visit. He'd left a pool cue on top of the table, along with the cue ball and one or two of its fellows. A small brandy snifter stood on a leather-topped table beside one of the big chairs. It was empty, but a quick sniff revealed it had recently held cognac—a very good cognac at that, judging from the bouquet.

There was a book next to the snifter, *Sheridan's Plays*, bound in red leather. Bedtime reading.

I went to the bookshelves. Had Arkwright inspected the little green clothbound volume as part of his nightly ritual? I couldn't tell, as it was right where I'd found it

earlier in the evening. But it was his treasure. He'd probably had a look at it.

I took it from the shelf and just managed to fit it into
my jacket pocket. Then I nudged the surrounding volumes so as to fill up the space where it had been.

And left the library.

ᘒᘓᘒ

He had turned off the alarm to enter the house, then
reset it once he and Elfrida were inside. All the while, of
course, the alarm system continued to guard all of the
house but the kitchen door. I now left through that very
portal, closing it after me and relocking its three locks by
picking them in reverse. I had to leave the chain bolt
dangling and I couldn't do anything about the bold I'd
hacksawed earlier. Nobody's perfect.

I was very damned close to perfection, though, in the
way I restored the alarm system, rewiring it to render
the kitchen door once more unbreachable. Every impulse urged me to quit Arkwright's property while I had
the chance, but I spent a few extra minutes, and only an
imperceptible scrap of electrical tape hinted that the
wires had ever been tampered with.

Professionalism? I call it the relentless pursuit of ex-
cellence.

ᘒᘓᘒ

I had almost reached the end of Copperwood Crescent when the police car turned the corner. I managed to
furnish a smile and a perfunctory nod without breaking
stride. They went along their merry way, and why not?

They'd seen only a well-dressed and self-possessed gentleman who looked as though he belonged.

They hadn't seen any palmless rubber gloves. Those wound up tucked in a pocket before I left the Arkwright driveway.

The Pontiac was where I'd left it. I hooked up my jumper wire and was on my way. In due course I was back on West Seventy-fourth Street. One nice thing about swiping a car from a hydrant is you can generally put it back where you found it. I did just that, pulling in next to the fireplug even as a brindle boxer was lifting a leg against it. I unhooked my jumper wire and got out of the car, careful to push down the lock buttons before I swung the door shut.

The boxer's equally brindle owner, leash in one hand and wad of paper towel in the other, admonished me that I was risking a ticket or a tow. I couldn't think of an answer so I walked off without giving him one.

"Crazy," he told the dog. "They're all crazy here, Max."

I couldn't argue with that.

In my own apartment, nibbling cheese and crunching Triscuits and sipping the special-occasion Scotch, I let go and enjoyed the glow that comes afterward on those too-rare occasions where everything goes like clockwork. All the tension, all the discomfort, all the anxiety—it was all bought and paid for by moments like this.

Earlier, stretched out on that lumpy day bed, I'd been unable to stop thinking of all the treasures the Arkwright house contained. The cash, the jewels, the stamps, the coins, the *objets d'art*. I'd had fantasies of backing a moving van onto the lawn and just stealing every damned thing, from the oriental rugs on the floors to the cut-crystal chandeliers overhead. That, I'd decided, was really the only way to do it. A person who wanted to be selective would have his problems. He wouldn't know what to steal first.

And what did I have for my troubles?

I picked up the book, taking pains not to dribble Scotch on it, though someone had dribbled one thing or another on it over the years. It certainly didn't look like such a much, and the leisurely inspection I could give it now was disclosing flaws I hadn't spotted earlier. There was water damage on the front cover. Some of the pages had been foxed. The past half-century had not been gentle with the little volume, and no bookseller could conscientiously grade it higher than Very Good.

I flipped through it, read a stanza here and a stanza there. The author's meter was unmistakable and he had never lost his dexterity at rhyming, but what I was reading looked like doggerel to me.

For this I'd passed up Krugerrands and Barber Proofs, Fabergé and Baccarat and Daum Nancy. For this I'd returned the pearl-and-ruby ring to its little velvet case.

Mr. Whelkin would be proud of me.

FOUR

I MET J. RUDYARD WHELKIN on a slow mid-week morning two weeks prior to my little venture in breaking and entering. The Yankees had just dropped the first two games of the Series, and the night before I'd watched a kid barely old enough to shave strike out Reggie Jackson with the bases loaded. This morning it was damp and drizzly, and it figured.

I hadn't had any customers yet and I didn't much care. I was settled in behind the counter with a paperback. I don't stock paperbacks, and the ones that come in I wholesale to a guy on Third and Sixteenth who deals in nothing else.

Sometimes, though, I read them first. The one I was reading was one of Richard Stark's books about Parker. Parker's a professional thief, and every book runs pretty much to form—Parker puts together a string of crooks, he goes someplace like Spartanburg, South Carolina, to buy guns and a truck, he gets a dentist in Yankton Falls to put up front money for the operation, he and his buddies pull the job, and then something goes horribly wrong. If nothing went horribly wrong, all of the books would end around page 70 and by now Parker would own his own island in the Caribbean.

Last time I was inside, everybody was a big fan of Parker's. My colleagues read everything they could get their hands on about him, even if they had to move their lips to get the job done. I swear there were grizzled cons in that joint who would walk around quoting passages at each other, especially parts where Parker maimed someone. One safecracker always quoted the part where Parker settled a score with an unworthy fellow laborer by breaking three important bones and leaving him in a swamp. It was the adjective that did it for him, the idea of deliberately breaking important bones.

I had just reached the part where Parker was putting in an urgent call to Handy McKay at his diner in Presque Isle, Maine, when the little bells above the door tinkled to announce I had company. I moved the paperback out of sight as my visitor approached the counter. After all, antiquarian booksellers have an image to protect. We're not supposed to read trash.

He was a stout man, florid of face, jowly as a bulldog, with thinning mahogany hair combed straight back over a glossy salmon scalp. He wore a charcoal-brown her-ringbone tweed jacket with suede elbow patches, a to-bacco-brown sweater vest, a tan oxford-cloth shirt with a button-down collar, a chocolate-brown knit tie. His trousers were fawn cavalry twill, his shoes brown wing tips. He had a long narrow nose, a graying guardsman's mustache. His eyebrows were untamed tangles of briar; beneath them his eyes (brown, to match his outfit) were keen and cool and just a trifle bloodshot.

He asked if Mr. Litzauer was expected, and I explained about the change in ownership. "Ah," he said. "No wonder he hasn't been in touch. I'm a collector, you see, and he always lets me know when he runs across an item I might fancy."

"What do you collect?"

"Victorian poets, for the most part, but I follow my taste, you know. I'm partial to artful rhymers. Thomas

Hood. Algernon Charles Swinburne. William Mackworth Praed. Kipling, of course, is my keenest enthusiasm."

I told him whatever I had was on the shelves. He went to look for himself and I got Parker out from beneath the counter and returned to vicarious crime. Two of Parker's henchpersons were just getting ready to set up a doublecross when my tweedy customer presented himself once again at the counter, a small cloth-bound volume in hand. It contained the collected lyric poems of Austin Dobson and I had it priced at six or seven dollars, something like that. He paid in cash and I wrapped it for him.

"If you happen on anything you think I might like," he said, "you might want to ring me up."

He handed me his card. It bore his name, an address in the East Thirties, and a phone number with a MUrray Hill 8 exchange. The card conveyed no suggestion of what the man did for a living.

I looked from it to him. "You collect Kipling," I said.

"Among others, yes."

"Is there a family connection?"

He smiled broadly. "Because of the name, you mean? Natural guess, of course. But no, I'm no relative of Kipling's. Rudyard's not a family name, you see. It's the name of a lake."

"Oh?"

"In Staffordshire. Kipling's parents first met on a picnic at Lake Rudyard. When in due course their son was born he was given the lake's name as a middle name. His first name was Joseph, actually, although he never did use it and was known as Ruddy from earliest childhood."

"And your first name—"

"Is James, as it happens, and I don't use it either. James Rudyard Whelkin. I was eight years old when Kipling died and I remember the day very well. That was in 1936, just two days after George V preceded him to the grave. A day of mourning in our household, as you can well imagine. My father admired Kipling enormously. He'd have to have done, to name his only son after him, wouldn't he? Because I was named for Kipling, of course, not for a lake in Staffordshire. 'First the old king and now the Bard of Empire,' my father said. 'Mark my words, Ruddy. There'll be war in Europe within the next two years.' He was off by a year of course, and I don't suppose Kipling's demise had much to do with Hitler's invading Poland, but it all linked up in the old fellow's mind, you see." He smiled fiercely and his great eyebrows shook. "Are you interested in Kipling, Mr. Rhodenbarr?"

"I read him when I was a kid."

"You might try him again. He's returning to fashion, you know, after altogether too many years of neglect. Have you had a look at *Kim* lately? Or *The Light That Failed*? Or—But reading must be a bit of a busman's holiday for you, eh? Must grow sick and tired of the printed word by the end of a long day."

"Oh, I still enjoy reading. And maybe I will try Kipling again."

"Do. There's books on your own shelves, for a starter." An appraising glance from his alert brown eyes. "I say, sir. Do you suppose you could possibly lunch with me this afternoon? I might have something to say that would interest you."

"I'd like that."

"My club, then. Do you know the Martingale? And how's half past twelve?"

I told him I knew where the club was, and that
twelve-thirty was fine.

He'd already said something that interested me.

The Martingale Club was just right for him, a good
match for his dress and his faintly pukka sahib manner.
It stood at the corner of Madison Avenue and Thirtieth
Street and was decorated largely with uncomfortable Jac-
obean oak furniture and the heads of innumerable dead
animals.

We dined in a fair-sized room on the second floor under the glass-eyed stare of a bison allegedly shot by Theo-
dore Roosevelt for reasons I could not begin to guess.
Lunch was a leathery mixed grill with thawed green peas
and spineless French fried potatoes. The waiter who
brought this mess to the table was a rheumy-eyed chap
who walked as though his feet were killing him. He
looked almost as woebegone as the bison.

Whelkin and I talked books through the meal, then
both turned down dessert. The sad waiter brought us a
large silver coffeepot of the sort they used to serve you
on trains. The coffee was even better than the old
Pennsy dining car once supplied, rich and winy and aro-
matic.

Our table was next to a pair of casement windows. I
sipped my coffee and looked out at Madison Avenue.
The last of the Good Humor men was doing light business on the corner. In a matter of days he'd be gone,
yielding place to a seller of hot pretzels and chestnuts as
the seasons changed in their inexorable fashion. You
couldn't watch the leaves turn, not from this window,

but you could mark time's passage by keeping an eye on the street vendors.

Whelkin cleared his throat, interrupting this reverie. "H. Rider Haggard," he said. "I told you I collect him as well?"

"I think you mentioned him."

"Interesting man. Did for South Africa what Kipling did for India. *She, King Solomon's Mines*—but of course you know his work."

"In a general way."

"He and Kipling became great friends, you know. Both of them were on the outs with the Bloomsbury crowd. Both lived long enough to see their own literary reputations fade dismally. The public came to think of them in the same breath as apologists for a discredited imperialism. Do you know the J. K. Stephens poem?"

I didn't even know whom he was talking about, but he managed to quote the poem from memory:

*"Will there never come a season
Which shall rid us from the curse
Of a prose which knows no reason
And an unmelodious verse:
When the world shall cease to wonder
At the genius of an Ass,
And a boy's eccentric blunder
Shall not bring success to pass:
When mankind shall be delivered
From the clash of magazines,
And the inkstand shall be shivered
Into countless smithereens:
When there stands a muzzled stripling,
Mute, beside a muzzled bore:
When the Rudyards cease from Kipling
And the Haggards Ride no more."*

He moved to refill our coffee cups. "Nasty piece of billingsgate, eh? One of many such. Just drove the two of them closer together, however. Haggard spent as much time at Kipling's house in Surrey as he did at home. They'd actually work together in Kipling's study, sitting on opposite ends of the long desk, batting ideas back and forth, then scribbling away furiously at one thing or another."

"Interesting," I said.

"Isn't it? Not too long after the 1918 Armistice the two men set about organizing the Liberty League, a sort of anti-Communist affair which never got terribly far off the ground. The bit of doggerel someone wrote gives a fair idea of the Liberty League's slant on current affairs. You know the poem?"

"I don't think so."

"It's cleverly rhymed, and I think I mentioned my admiration for a facility at rhyming.

" *'Every Bolsh is a blackguard,'*
Said Kipling to Haggard.
'And given to tippling,'
Said Haggard to Kipling.
'And a blooming outsider,'
Said Rudyard to Rider.
'Their domain is a bloodyard,'
Said Rider to Rudyard.

"Neatly done, don't you think? I could quote others of a similar nature but I'll spare you that."

I very nearly thanked him. I was beginning to think I'd been mistaken, that he'd just brought me here to quote verse at me. Well, at least the coffee was good.

Then he said, "Liberty League. After it fell apart,

Kipling went through a difficult time. His health was poor. Gastritis, which he thought might be symptomatic of cancer. Turned out he had duodenal ulcers. He was subject to depression and it may have affected his thinking.

"The man became briefly fixated on the curious notion that the British Empire was menaced by an unholy alliance of Jewish international financiers and Jewish Bolsheviks. These two unlikely forces were joining together to destroy Christianity by wresting the overseas empire from the British crown. Kipling wasn't the sort of moral degenerate to whom anti-Semitism comes naturally, and he didn't persist in it for any length of time, nor did it color his work to a considerable extent.

"But he did write one extremely bizarre piece of work on an anti-Semitic theme. It was a narrative poem in ballad meter, some three thousand two hundred lines called *The Deliverance of Fort Bucklow*. The plot line concerns the efforts of a gallant British regiment to save India from a revolution stirred up by Jewish agitators, and it's quite clear that the battle for Fort Bucklow is not merely the decisive battle of this war but Kipling's version of the Battle of Armageddon, with the forces of Good and Evil pitted against one another to decide the fate of humankind.

"Do you remember *Soldiers Three*? Learoyd, Ortheris and Mulvaney? Kipling brought them back to make them the heroes who deliver Fort Bucklow and save the day for God and King George. Oh, there are some stirring battle scenes, and there's a moment when 'two brave men stand face to face' in a manner reminiscent of *The Ballad of East and West*, but poor Kipling was miles from the top of his form when he wrote it. The premise is absurd, the resolution is weak, and there are elements of frightful unwitting self-parody. He often skated rather close to the edge of self-parody, you know, and here he lost his footing.

"Perhaps he recognized this himself. Perhaps his vision of the Hebraic Conspiracy embraced the world of publishing. In any event, he didn't offer *The Deliverance of Fort Bucklow* to his London publishers. He may have planned to do so ultimately, but in the meantime he elected to safeguard the copyright by bringing out the poem in a small private edition."

"Ah."

"Ah indeed, sir. Kipling found a printer named Smithwick & Son in Tunbridge Wells. If Smithwick ever printed another book before or since, I've never heard of it. But he did print this one, and in an edition of only one hundred fifty copies. It's not fine printing by any means because Smithwick wasn't capable of it. But he got the job done, and the book's quite a rarity."

"It must be. One hundred fifty copies . . ."

Whelkin smiled widely. "That's how many were printed. How many do you suppose survive?"

"I have no idea. *The Deliverance of Fort Bucklow?* I've never heard the title."

"I'm not surprised."

"Fifty copies? Seventy-five? I have no idea what the survival rate would be."

The coffeepot was empty. Whelkin frowned and rang a bell mounted on the wall. He didn't say anything until the waiter limped over with a fresh pot.

Then he said, "Kipling wrote the poem in 1923. He'd hoped to give out copies to close friends for Christmas that year, but the holiday had come and gone before Smithwick was able to make delivery. So Kipling decided to hold them over for Christmas of '24, but sometime in the course of the year he seems to have come to his senses, recognizing the poem as a scurrilous piece of Jew-baiting tripe and bad verse in the bargain.

"As was his custom, Kipling had presented his wife, Carrie, with an inscribed copy. He asked for it back. He'd given another copy to a Surrey neighbor of his named Lonsdale as a birthday gift in early spring and he managed to get it back as well, giving the man several other books in exchange. These two books, as well as the other bound volumes, the printer's proofs, and the original holograph manuscript plus the typed manuscript from which Smithwick set type—all of this went up the chimney at Bateman's."

"Bateman's?"

"Bateman's was the name of Kipling's house. There's an undated letter to a London acquaintance, evidently written in the late summer or early fall of '24, in which Kipling talks of having felt like an erring Israelite who had just sacrificed a child by fire to Moloch. 'But this was a changeling, this bad child of mine, and it was with some satisfaction I committed it to the flames.' " Whelkin sighed with contentment, sipped coffee, placed his cup in its saucer. "And that," he said, "was the end of *The Deliverance of Fort Bucklow.*"

"Except that it wasn't."

"Of course not, Mr. Rhodenbarr. The Rider Haggard copy still existed. Kipling, of course, had given a copy to his closest friend almost as soon as he received the edition from Smithwick. Had it slipped his mind when he set about recalling the other copies? I don't think so.

"Haggard, you see, was in failing health. And Kipling had dedicated the book to Haggard, and had added a personal inscription to Haggard's own copy, a paragraph running to over a hundred words in which he hailed Haggard as a kindred spirit who shared the author's vision of the peril of Jewish-inspired holocaust, or words to that effect. I believe there's a letter of Rider Haggard's in the collection of the University of Texas acknowledging the gift and praising the poem. After all that, Kipling may have been understandably reluctant to disown the work and ask for the book's return. In any event, the copy was still in Haggard's possession upon his death the following year."

"Then what happened to it?"

"It was sold along with the rest of Haggard's library, and no one seems to have paid any immediate attention to it. The world didn't know the book existed, and no doubt it was sold in a lot with the other copies of Kipling's works, and for very little money, I'm sure. It came to light shortly after Kipling's death—not the copy, but the realization that Kipling had written an anti-Semitic poem. The British Union of Fascists wanted to disseminate it, and Unity Mitford was rumored to have been on the trail of the Haggard copy when war broke out between Britain and Germany.

"Nothing further was heard until after the war, when the Haggard copy turned up in the possession of a North Country baronet, who sold it privately. There were supposed to have been two or three additional private transactions before the volume was scheduled to appear in Trebizond & Partners auction of effects from the estate of the twelfth Lord Ponsonby."

"You say scheduled to appear?"

He nodded shortly. "Scheduled, catalogued and withdrawn. Six weeks ago I took one of Freddie Laker's no-frills flights to London with the sole purpose of bidding on that book. I calculated that the competition would be keen. There are some rabid Kipling collectors, you know, and his reputation's been making a comeback. The University of Texas has a well-endowed library and their Kipling collection is a sound one. I expected there would be buyers for other institutions as well."

"Did you expect to outbid them?"

"I expected to try. I didn't know just how high I myself was prepared to go, and of course I had no way of knowing what levels the bidding might reach. Upon arriving in London, I learned there was a Saudi who wanted that particular lot, and rumor had it that an agent for some sort of Indian prince or Maharajah was paying extraordinary prices for top-level Kiplingana. Could I have outbid such persons? I don't know. *The Deliverance of Fort Bucklow* is interesting and unique, but it hasn't been publicized sufficiently to have become *important*, really, and the work itself is of low quality from a literary standpoint." He frowned, and his eyebrows quivered. "Still in all, I should have liked the chance to bid in open auction."

"But the lot was withdrawn."

"By the heirs prior to sale. The gentleman from Trebizond's was quite apologetic, and reasonably indignant himself. After all, his agreement with the heirs precluded their making private agreements. But what could he possibly do about it? The buyer had the book and the heirs had the money and that was the end of it."

"Why arrange a private sale?"

"Taxes, Mr. Rhodenbarr. Taxes. Death duties, Inland Revenue enquiries—the tax laws make finaglers of us all, do they not? What voice on earth speaks with the volume of unrecorded cash? Money in hand, passed under the table, and the heirs can swear the book was set aside as an heirloom, or destroyed in a flash flood, or whatever they choose. They won't be believed, but what matter?"

"Who bought the book?"

"The good people at Trebizond's didn't know, of course. And the heirs weren't telling—their official line was that the book hadn't been sold at all." He put his elbows on the table and placed his fingertips together. "I did some investigatory work of my own. *The Deliverance of Fort Bucklow* was sold to Jesse Arkwright, an artful dabbler in international trade."

"And a collector, I suppose?"

"An acquirer, sir. Not a collector. A gross ill-favored man who surrounds himself with exquisite objects in the hope that they will somehow cloak his own inner ugliness. He has a library, Mr. Rhodenbarr, because to do so fits the image he would like to project. He has books, some of them noteworthy, because books are the *sine qua non* of a proper library. But he is hardly a collector, and he most certainly does not collect Kipling."

"Then why—"

"Should he want this book? Because *I* wanted it, Mr. Rhodenbarr. It's that simple."

"Oh."

"Do you remember the Spinning Jenny?"

"It was a dance craze, wasn't it?"

He looked at me oddly. "It was a machine," he said. "The first machine capable of producing cotton thread. Sir Richard Arkwright patented it in 1769 and launched the modern British textile industry."

"Oh, right," I said. "The Industrial Revolution and all that."

"And all that," he agreed. "Jesse Arkwright claims descent from Sir Richard. I'm no more inclined to take his word on that point than any other. His surname

means *builder of arks*, so perhaps he'll next hire a gene-
alogist to trace his roots clear back to Noah."

"And he bought the book to keep you from having
it?"

"I once acquired something that he wanted. This
seems to have been his way of paying me back."

"And he won't sell it."

"Certainly not."

"And there's no other copy extant."

"None has come to light in half a century."

"And you still want this particular copy."

"More than ever."

"How fortunate that you happened to pop into Barnegat Books this morning."

He stared.

"You called me by name before I had a chance to
supply it. You came into the shop looking for me, not for
Mr. Litzauer. Not because I sell secondhand books but
because I used to be a burglar. You figure I'm still a burglar."

"I—"

"You don't believe people change. You're as bad as
the police. 'Once a burglar, always a burglar'—that's the
way you figure it, isn't it?"

"I was wrong," he said, and lowered his eyes.

"No," I said. "You were right."

FIVE

I DON'T KNOW what time I got into bed, but by some
miracle I got out of it in time to open the store by ten-
thirty. At a quarter to eleven I called the number on J.
Rudyard Whelkin's business card. I let it ring unheeded
for a full minute, then dialed 411 for the number of the
Martingale Club. They charged you for those calls, and I
could have taken a minute to look it up in the White
Pages, but I'd earned a fortune the night before and I felt
like sharing the wealth.

The attendant at the Martingale Club said he didn't
believe Mr. Whelkin was on the premises but that he'd
page him all the same. Time scuttled by. The attendant
reported mournfully that Mr. Whelkin had not responded to the page, and would I care to leave a message? I decided not to.

A couple of browsers filtered into the store. One of
them looked potentially larcenous and I kept an eye on
him as he worked his way through Biography and Belles-
Lettres. He surprised me in the end by spending a few
dollars on a volume of Macaulay's historical essays.

Carolyn popped in a few minutes after noon and de-
posited a paper bag on the counter. "Felafel sandwiches
on pita bread," she announced. "I decided I was in the
mood for something different. You like felafel?"

"Sure."

"I went to that place at the corner of Broadway and

Twelfth. I can't figure out whether the owner's an Arab or an Israeli."

"Does it matter?"

"Well, I'd hate to say the wrong thing. I was going to wish him a happy Rosh Hashanah, but suppose that's the last thing he wants to hear? So I just took my change and split."

"That's always safe."

"Uh-huh. You missed a terrific meal last night. I ate half the stew and froze the rest and started watching the new sitcom about the three cheerleaders. I turned the sound off and it wasn't half bad. But I got to bed early and I got a ton of sleep and I feel great."

"You look it."

"You, on the other hand, look terrible. Is that what a night on club soda does to a person?"

"Evidently."

"Maybe you got too much sleep. That happens sometimes."

"So they tell me."

The phone rang. I went and took it in the little office in back, figuring it was Whelkin. Instead it was a slightly breathless woman who wanted to know if the new Rosemary Rogers book had come in yet. I told her I handled used books exclusively and suggested she call Brentano's. She asked what their number was and I was reaching for the phone book to look it up when I came to my senses and hung up on her.

I went back to my felafel. Carolyn said, "Something wrong?"

"No. Why?"

"You jumped three feet when the phone rang. The coffee okay?"

"Fine."

"The felafel?"

"Delicious."

Mondays and Wednesdays I buy lunch and we eat at the Poodle Factory. Tuesdays and Thursdays Carolyn brings lunch to the bookshop. Fridays we go out somewhere and toss a coin for the check. All of this is subject to last-minute cancellation, of course, in the event of a business luncheon, such as my earlier date with Whelkin.

"Oh," I said, and finished swallowing a mouthful of felafel. "I haven't squandered the morning."

"I never said you had."

"I did some research. On patron saints."

"Oh yeah? Who's my patron saint?"

"I don't think you've got one."

"Why the hell not?"

"I don't know. I checked a lot of different books and kept finding partial lists. I don't know if there's an official all-inclusive list anywhere." I groped around, found the notepad I'd been scribbling on earlier. "I told you about St. John of God, didn't I?"

"Yeah, but I forget what. The store?"

"Patron saint of booksellers. He was born in Portugal in 1495. He worked as a shepherd, then became a drunkard and gambler."

"Good for him. Then he switched to club soda and became a saint."

"The books don't say anything about club soda. At forty he went through a mid-life crisis and moved to Granada. In 1538 he opened a shop—"

"To sell books?"

"I suppose so, but did they have bookstores then? They barely had movable type. Anyway, two years later he founded the Brothers Hospitalers, and ten years later he died, and his picture's hanging over my desk, if you'd care to see it."

"Not especially. That's all you found out?"

"Not at all." I consulted my notes. "You asked if there was a patron saint of burglars. Well, Dismas is the patron saint of thieves. He was the Good Thief."

"Yeah, I remember him."

"He's also one of the patron saints of prisoners, along with St. Joseph Cafasso. Thieves and prisoners do overlap, although not as thoroughly as you might think."

"And prisoners need an extra patron saint because they're in real trouble."

"Makes sense. A burglar's a thief, when all is said and done, and there doesn't seem to be a special burglar's saint, but there's always St. Dunstan."

"Who he?"

"The patron saint of locksmiths. Burglars and locksmiths perform essentially the same task, so why shouldn't they both turn to Dunstan in time of stress? Of course, if the situation's really dire, a burglar could turn to St. Jude Thaddeus or St. Gregory of Neocaesarea."

"Why would he want to do that?"

"Because those guys are the patron saints of persons in desperate situations. There were times in my burglar days when I could have used their help. For that matter, I didn't know about St. Anthony of Padua, the patron saint of seekers of lost objects."

"So if you couldn't find what you were looking for . . ."

"Precisely. You're laughing. That means I should give thanks to St. Vitus."

"The patron saint of dancers?"

"Comedians, actually. Dancers have somebody else, but don't ask me who."

"What about dog groomers?"

"I'll have to consult more sources."

"And lesbians. You honestly couldn't find anything about lesbians?"

"Well, there's somebody who comes to mind. But I don't know his name and I don't think he was a saint."

"Lesbians have a male saint?"

"He's probably not a saint anyway."

"Well, don't keep me in suspense. Who is he?"

"That little Dutch boy."

"*What* little Dutch boy?"

"You know. The one who put his finger—"

"Nobody likes a smartass, Bernie. Not even St. Vitus."

❧❧❧

The afternoon sped by without further reference to patron saints. I racked up a string of small sales and moved a nice set of Trollope to a fellow who'd been sniffing around it for weeks. He wrote out a check for sixty bucks and staggered off with the books in his arms.

Whenever I had a minute I called Whelkin without once reaching him. When he didn't answer the page at the Martingale Club, I left a message for him to call Mr. Haggard. I figured that would be subtle enough.

The phone rang around four. I said, "Barnegat Books?" and nobody said anything for a moment. I figured I had myself a heavy breather, but for the hell of it I said, "Mr. Haggard?"

"Sir?"

It was Whelkin, of course. And he hadn't gotten my

message, having been away from home and club all day long. His speech was labored, with odd pauses between the sentences. An extra martini at lunch, I figured.

"Could you pop by this evening, Mr. Rhodenbarr?"

"At your club?"

"No, that won't be convenient. Let me give you my address."

"I already have it."

"How's that?"

"You gave me your card," I reminded him, and read off the address to him.

"Won't be there tonight," he said shortly. He sounded as though someone had puffed up his tongue with a bicycle pump. He went on to give me an address on East Sixty-sixth between First and Second avenues. "Apartment 3-D," he said. "Ring twice."

"Like the postman."

"Beg pardon?"

"What time should I come?"

He thought it over. "Half past six, I should think."

"That's fine."

"And you'll bring the, uh, the item?"

"If you'll have the, uh, cash."

"Everything will be taken care of."

Odd, I thought, hanging up the phone. I was the one running on four hours' sleep. He was the one who sounded exhausted.

જાર્જ

I don't know exactly when the Sikh appeared. He was just suddenly there, poking around among the shelves, a tall slender gentleman with a full black beard and a turban. I noticed him, of course, because one does notice that sort of thing, but I didn't stare or gawp. New York is New York, after all, and a Sikh is not a Martian.

Shortly before five the store emptied out. I stifled a yawn with the back of my hand and thought about closing early. Just then the Sikh emerged from the world of books and presented himself in front of the counter. I'd lost track of him and had assumed he'd left.

"This book," he said. He held it up for my inspection, dwarfing it in his large brown hands. An inexpensive copy of *The Jungle Book*, by our boy Rudyard K.

"Ah, yes," I said. "Mowgli, raised by wolves."

He was even taller than I'd realized. I looked at him and thought of What's-his-name in Little Orphan Annie. He wore a gray business suit, a white shirt, an unornamented maroon tie. The turban was white.

"You know this man?"

Punjab, I thought. That was the dude in Little Orphan Annie. And his sidekick was The Asp, and—

"Kipling?" I said.

"You know him?"

"Well, he's not living now," I said. "He died in 1936." And thank you, J. R. Whelkin, for the history lesson.

The man smiled. His teeth were very large, quite even, and whiter than his shirtfront. His features were regular, and his large sorrowful eyes were the brown of old-fashioned mink coats, the kind Ray Kirschmann's wife didn't want for Christmas.

"You know his books?" he said.

"Yes."

"You have other books, yes? Besides the ones on your shelves."

An alarm bell sounded somewhere in the old cerebellum. "My stock's all on display," I said carefully.

"Another book. A private book, perhaps."

"I'm afraid not."

The smile faded until the mouth was a grim line hidden at its corners by the thick black beard. The Sikh dropped a hand into his jacket pocket. When he brought it out there was a pistol in it. He stood so that his body screened the pistol from the view of passers-by and held it so that it was pointed directly at my chest.

It was a very small gun, a nickel-plated automatic. They make fake guns about that size, novelty items, but somehow I knew that this one wouldn't turn out to be a cigarette lighter in disguise.

It should have looked ridiculous, such a little gun in such a large hand, but I'll tell you something. Guns, when they're pointed at me, never look ridiculous.

"Please," he said patiently. "Let us be reasonable. You know what I want."

SIX

I wanted to look him in the eyes but I couldn't keep from staring at the gun.

"There is something," I said.

"Yes."

"I've got it behind the counter, see, because of a personal interest—"

"Yes."

"But since you're a fan of Kipling's, and because your devotion is obvious—"

"The book, please."

His free hand snatched it up the instant I laid it on the counter. The smile was back now, broader than ever. He tried the book in his jacket pocket but it didn't fit. He set it back on the counter for a moment while he drew an envelope from an inside pocket. He was still pointing the gun at me and I wished he'd stop.

"For your trouble," he said, slapping the envelope smartly on the counter in front of me. "Because you are a reasonable man."

"Reasonable," I said.

"No police, no troubles." His smile spread. "Reasonable."

"Like Brutus."

"I beg your pardon?"

"No, he was honorable, wasn't he? And I'm reasonable." The book screamed at me from the counter top.

"This book," I said, my hand pawing the air above it. "You're a stranger in my country, and I can't let you—"

He scooped up the book and backed off, teeth flashing furiously. When he reached the door he pocketed the gun, stepped quickly outside, and hurried off westward on Eleventh Street.

Gone but not forgotten.

I stared after him for a moment or two. Then I suppose I sighed, and finally I picked up the envelope and weighed it in my hand as if trying to decide how many stamps to put on it. It was a perfectly ordinary envelope of the sort doctors mail their bills in, except that there was no return address in its upper left-hand corner. Just a simple blank envelope, dime-store stationery.

Rudyard Whelkin had agreed to pay me fifteen thousand dollars for the book he wanted. Somehow I couldn't make myself believe this little envelope contained fifteen thousand dollars.

I opened it. Fifty-dollar bills, old ones, out of sequence.

Ten of them.

Five hundred dollars.

Big hairy deal.

I dragged the bargain table in from the street. Somehow I wasn't eager to stay open a few extra minutes in order to peddle a few old books at three for a buck. I hung the *Closed* sign in the window and set about shutting things down, transferring some cash from the register to my wallet, filling out a deposit slip for the check I'd taken in on the Trollope set.

I folded the ten fifties and buttoned them into a hip

pocket. And snatched up a brown-wrapped book from a drawer in the office desk, and let myself out of the store and went through my nightly lockup routine with the steel gates.

For a few minutes I just walked, north on Broadway, then east on Thirteenth Street, then uptown on Third Avenue. The corner of Fourteenth and Third was aswarm with persons addicted to any of a variety of licit and illicit substances. Junkies scratched themselves, winos passed pints around, and a methadone enthusiast kept slamming the heel of his hand thoughtfully against a brick building. I straightened the knot in my tie—I'd put the tie on before leaving the store—and walked onward, resisting the temptation to give my hip pocket a reassuring pat.

Five hundred dollars.

There's a big difference between five hundred and fifteen thousand, and while the latter sum represents a very decent return on a night's labor, the former is small compensation for risking life and limb, not to mention liberty. So a five-hundred-dollar payment for *The Deliverance of Fort Bucklow* was like no money at all.

On the other hand, five hundred dollars was a princely sum for the Grosset & Dunlap reprint edition of *Soldiers Three*, which is what my turbaned and bearded visitor had taken from me at gunpoint. I rather doubt it was what he wanted, but you don't always get what you want, do you?

I'd had the book priced reasonably enough at $1.95. And I had the Haggard copy of *The Deliverance of Fort Bucklow* all nicely wrapped in brown kraft paper and tucked under my arm, and wouldn't Rudyard Whelkin be happy to see it?

It's funny how things work out.

SEVEN

I WAS EARLY, of course. My appointment with Whelkin wasn't until six-thirty and I'd locked up the shop just a few minutes after five, not wanting to stick around in case the Sikh realized his mistake. I had a sign on the wall emphasizing that all sales were final, but I had a feeling he'd expect me to make an exception in his case. So I took my time walking uptown, and I was still twenty minutes early when I reached the corner of Sixty-sixth and Second. A bar on the corner looked inviting, and I accepted the invitation.

I don't drink when I'm working. But this wasn't exactly work, and I'd felt the need for something after staring into the barrel of the Sikh's automatic. As a matter of fact, I'd stopped for a quick bracer in a Third Avenue ginmill on my way uptown. Now I wanted something a little more civilized, a dry Rob Roy in a stemmed and frosted glass.

I sipped it and did a little thinking, ticking off points on my fingers.

Point One: Only J. Rudyard Whelkin had known I was going to steal the book from the Arkwright house in Forest Hills Gardens.

Point Two: It was four o'clock before Whelkin knew I had the book. He'd known I was going there, but there's many a slip between the cup and the whatsit, and it wasn't until he called me at the bookstore that he knew for certain my trip to Queens had paid off. In all likelihood, Arkwright himself didn't even know the book was missing yet.

Point Three: The Sikh had not been a bizarre coincidence, one of those phenomena that make life the ever-exciting proposition it indisputably is. No way. The Sikh had darkened my doorway because he knew I had stolen Arkwright's copy of *The Deliverance of Fort Bucklow.*

Hard work, thinking. I checked my watch, took another sip of my Rob Roy.

Assumption: The Sikh did not have mystical powers. He knew I had the book because the information had somehow reached him via Whelkin.

Hypothesis: J. Rudyard Whelkin was as reluctant as the next skinflint to part with fifteen grand. Once he'd established that I had the book in my possession, he simply dispatched his faithful native servant to fetch it for him, instructing him to slip me the ten fifties to smooth my ruffled feathers.

The hypothesis had me clenching my teeth and making a fist at the very thought. I had a little more of my Rob Roy and did some deep breathing.

Rebuttal: The hypothesis didn't make sense. If Whelkin was going to rob me, why send someone to the store? He'd already taken pains to set up a meeting on East Sixty-sixth Street, where he could arrange an elaborate ambush with ease.

Alternate Hypothesis: The Sikh was somebody else's faithful native servant. Hadn't Whelkin mentioned that several parties had intended to bid on the book at Trebizond's London auction? Was it not possible that one of them had followed the book to New York, scheming to wrest it away from Arkwright's possession, only to see it whisked out from under his nose by one B. G. Rhoden-barr?

That seemed to make more sense, but it still left a stone or two unturned. I found myself wondering what would happen when the Sikh's employer took a look at *Soldiers Three*. The sooner I turned the book over to Whelkin and collected my fifteen thousand dollars, the better I'd be able to cope with him. The best way to cope, I felt, would be to take a quick vacation somewhere, spending a portion of the boodle and giving him time to cool off or leave town or, ideally, both.

I stood up.

And sat down again.

Did I have anything to fear from Whelkin? I was pretty sure he hadn't sent the Sikh, but suppose I was wrong? Or suppose he had not sent the Sikh and indeed knew nothing about the Sikh, but suppose he had his own ideas about doing me out of my fee? Was it possible I'd let myself be snowed by the elegant manner and the Martingale Club membership? The rich, I've noted, are no more eager to part with a bundle than anyone else. And here I was, meeting him on his own turf, bringing him the book like a dutiful dog with the evening paper in his mouth. Lord, I couldn't even testify that Whelkin *had* fifteen thousand dollars, let alone that he was prepared to hand it over to me.

I went to the men's room, book in hand. When I returned I had both hands free. The book was wedged under my belt against the small of my back, out of sight beneath my suit jacket.

I finished the last of my drink. I'd have liked another, but that could wait until the completion of my business transaction.

First things first.

⤳⟡⤳

The house on Sixty-sixth Street was an elegant brownstone with a plant-filled bay window on the parlor floor. Taller buildings stood on either side of it, but the old brownstone held its own. I walked up a half flight of stairs and studied a row of bells in the vestibule.

M. Porlock. 3-D.

I rang twice. Nothing happened for a moment and I checked my watch again. It said 6:29 and it is a watch that rarely lies. I placed my finger on the bell again, tentatively, and at that instant the answering buzzer sounded and I pushed the door open.

There were two apartments on the parlor floor, four each on the three floors above it. (The basement had its own entrance.) I mounted two flights of carpeted stairs with an increasing feeling of mingled anticipation and dread. The D apartments were at the rear of the building. The door of 3-D was slightly ajar. I gave it a rap with my knuckles and it was almost immediately drawn open by a square-shouldered woman wearing a muted-plaid skirt and a brass-buttoned navy blazer. Her dark-brown hair was very short and irregularly cut, as if the barber had been either a drunken friend or a very trendy beautician.

She said, "Mr. Rhodenbarr? Do come in."

"I was supposed to meet—"

"Ruddy Whelkin, I know. He's expected at any moment. He rang up not ten minutes ago to say he'd been momentarily detained." She smiled suddenly. "I'm to make you comfortable, you see. I'm Madeleine Porlock."

I took the hand she extended. "Bernie Rhodenbarr," I said. "But you already know that."

"Your reputation precedes you. Won't you have a seat? And may I get you a drink?"

"Not just now," I said. To the drink, that is; I seated myself in a tub chair upholstered in glove-soft green Naugahyde. The living room was small but comfortable, with a Victorian rosewood love seat and a floral-slip-covered easy chair in addition to the tub chair. The bold abstract oil over the love seat somehow complemented the furnishings. It was a nice room, and I said as much.

"Thank you. You're sure you won't have a little sherry?"

"I'll pass for now."

There was classical music playing on the radio, a woodwind ensemble that sounded like Vivaldi. Madeleine Porlock crossed the room, adjusted the volume. There was something familiar about her but I couldn't think what it was.

"Ruddy should be here any moment," she said again.

"Have you known him long?"

"Ruddy? Seems like ages."

I tried picturing them as a couple. They didn't bear mentioning in the same breath with Steve and Eydie, or even Bob and Carol and Ted and Alice, but they weren't utterly inconceivable. He was a good deal older than she, certainly. She looked to be in her early thirties, although I'm terrible at judging people's ages.

Did I know her from somewhere?

I was on the verge of asking when she clapped her hands together as if she'd just hit on the principle of specific gravity. "Coffee," she said.

"I beg your pardon?"

"You'll have a cup of coffee. It's freshly made. You will have some, won't you?"

I'd turned down the drink because I wanted to remain

alert. All the more reason to have the coffee. We agreed on cream and sugar and she went off to prepare it. I settled myself in the tub chair and listened to the music, thinking how nice it would be to be able to play the bassoon. I'd priced bassoons once and they cost a lot, and I understand the instrument's exceedingly difficult to learn, and I don't even remember how to read music, so I don't suppose I'll ever go so far as to acquire a bassoon and set about taking lessons, but whenever I hear the instrument in a concerto or a chamber work it occurs to me how nice it would be to go to sleep one night and wake up the following morning owning a bassoon and knowing how to play it.

Things go so much simpler in fantasy. You leave out all the scut work that way.

"Mr. Rhodenbarr?"

I took the coffee from her. She'd served it in a chunky earthenware mug ornamented with a geometric design. I sniffed at the coffee and allowed that it smelled good.

"I hope you like it," she said. "It's a Louisiana blend I've been using lately. It has chicory in it."

"I like chicory."

"Oh, so do I," she said. She made it sound as though our mutual enthusiasm could be the start of something big. The woodwind quintet ended—it *was* Vivaldi, according to the announcer—and a Haydn symphony replaced it.

I took a sip of my coffee. She asked if it was all right and I assured her that it was wonderful, although it really wasn't. There was a slight off-taste discernible beneath the cream and sugar, and I decided that chicory was one of those things I don't really like but just think I do.

"Ruddy said you were bringing him something, Mr. Rhodenbarr."

"Yes."

"He seemed very anxious about it. You have it with you, of course?"

I drank more coffee and decided that it wasn't really all that bad. The Haydn symphony rolled in waves, echoing within the little room.

"Mr. Rhodenbarr."

"Nice music," I said.

"Do you have the book, Mr. Rhodenbarr?"

I was smiling. I had the feeling it was a sort of dopey smile but I couldn't seem to do anything about it.

"Mr. Rhodenbarr?"

"You're very pretty."

"The book, Mr. Rhodenbarr."

"I know you from somewhere. You look familiar." I was spilling coffee on myself, for some reason, and I felt deeply embarrassed. I shouldn't have had that Rob Roy, I decided, and then Madeleine Porlock was taking the cup away from me and placing it carefully on the glass-topped coffee table.

"I always walk into those things," I confided. "Glass tables. Don't see them. Walk right into them. You have orange hair."

"Close your eyes, Mr. Rhodenbarr."

My eyes slammed shut. I pried them open and looked at her. She had a mop of curly orange hair, and as I stared at her it disappeared and her hair was short and dark again. I blinked, trying to make it orange, but it stayed as it was.

"The coffee," I said, brilliantly. "Something in the coffee."

"Sit back and relax, Mr. Rhodenbarr."

"You drugged me." I braced my hands on the arms of the chair and tried to stand. I couldn't even get my behind off the chair. My arms had no strength in them and my legs didn't even appear to exist anymore.

"Orange hair," I said.

"Close your eyes, Mr. Rhodenbarr."

"Have to get up—"

"Sit back and rest. You're very tired."

God, that was the truth. I gulped air, shook my head furiously in an attempt to shake some of the cobwebs loose. That was a mistake—the motion set off a string of tiny firecrackers somewhere in the back of my skull. Haydn dipped and soared. My eyes closed again, and I strained to get them open and saw her leaning over me, telling me how sleepy I was.

I kept my eyes open. Even so, my field of vision began to darken along its edges. Then patches of black appeared here and there, and they grew together until it was all black, everywhere, and I gave up and let go and fell all the way down to the bottom.

❧❧❧

I was dreaming something about an earthquake in Turkey, houses crumbling around me, boulders rolling down the sides of mountains. I fought my way out of the dream like an underwater swimmer struggling to reach the water's surface. The Turkish earthquake was part of the hourly newscast on the radio. The Social Democrats had scored substantial gains in parliamentary elections in Belgium. A Hollywood actor had died of an overdose of sleeping pills. The President was expected to veto something or other.

A buzzer was sounding nearby, interrupting the monotony of the newscast. I managed to open my eyes. My head ached and my mouth tasted as though I'd fallen asleep sucking the wad of cotton from the vitamin jar. The buzzer buzzed again and I wondered why nobody was answering it.

I opened my eyes again. Evidently they had closed without my knowing it. The radio announcer was inviting me to subscribe to *Backpacker Magazine*. I didn't want to but wasn't sure I had the strength to refuse. The buzzer was still buzzing. I wished Madeleine Porlock would get up from the Victorian love seat and answer it, or make them stop buzzing, or something.

The radio switched to music. Something with violins. Soothing. I opened my eyes again. The buzzing had stopped and there was the sound of heavy footsteps on the stairs.

I was still in the tub chair. My left hand lay in my lap like a small dead animal. My right arm was draped over the side of the chair, and there was something in my right hand.

I opened my eyes again, gave my head a shake. Something loose rattled around inside it. Someone was knocking on the door. I wished the Porlock woman would answer it, but she was in no better shape than I was.

They banged harder on the door and I opened my eyes again, and this time I managed to straighten up in the chair and kick through to something resembling actual consciousness. I gulped air and blinked rapidly and remembered where I was and what I was doing there.

I moved my left hand, reached around and felt the small of my back. *The Deliverance of Fort Bucklow* was gone.

Well, that figured.

"Open up in there!"

Knock, knock, knock, and I felt like the drunken porter in *Macbeth*. I called out for them to wait a minute and reached to check my hip pocket for the Sikh's five hundred dollars. I couldn't reach that pocket with my left hand. And why was I using my left, anyway? Oh, sure. Because there was something heavy in my right hand.

"Police! Open up in there!"

More furious pounding on the door. I raised my right hand. There was a gun in it. I stared stupidly at it, then raised it to my face and sniffed its muzzle. I smelled that particular mix of gun oil and gunpowder and burnt odor characteristic of a recently fired weapon.

I looked at the love seat again, hoping to find it empty, wishing what I'd seen earlier had been a mirage. But Madeleine Porlock was still there, and she hadn't moved, and I could see now that she wasn't likely to, not without more help than I could give her.

She'd been shot in the middle of the forehead, right where the horrid little girl had a little curl, and I had a fairly good idea what gun had done the deed.

EIGHT

I GOT UP quickly—too quickly—the blood rushed to my feet, or wherever it goes under such circumstances, and I very nearly fell back down again. But I stayed on my feet and fought to clear my head a little.

The radio was still playing. I wanted to turn it off but left it alone. The cops had left off knocking on the door and were slamming into it every few seconds. Any moment now the door would give and they'd come stumbling into the room.

I decided I didn't want to be there when that happened.

I was still holding the damned gun. I dropped it, and then I picked it up and wiped my prints off it, and then I dropped it again and made my way past the radio and through a short hallway with a bathroom and closet on one side and a pullman kitchen on the other. At the end of the hallway a door opened into a fair-sized bedroom furnished with a four-poster spool bed and a Pennsylvania Dutch blanket chest. There was a window on the far wall over the bed, and *it* opened onto a fire escape, and I damn well opened it.

Fresh air, cold fresh air. I filled both lungs and felt some of the cobwebs leave my brain. I climbed out onto the fire escape and closed the window after me. With it shut I could just barely hear the sounds of police officers caroming off the apartment door.

Now what?

I looked down and a wave of vertigo hit me. I thought of all the drug labels with their warnings about driving or operating machinery. *If drowsiness occurs, stay off rickety fire escapes.*

I took another look. Below me, the fire escape terminated in a courtyard walled off on all three sides. I might get into the basement, but there was sure to be a cop posted downstairs, most likely a fat one who hadn't wanted to climb up two flights in the first place.

So I started up the fire escape, up past the fourth floor and on to the roof. Someone had built a redwood sundeck up there, and there were trees and shrubs in large redwood planters. It was all very lovely, but there was one trouble with it—I couldn't get off it. The adjoining buildings were both a hundred or more feet taller than the one I was standing on, and the heavy fire door leading back into the building couldn't be opened without a key. This wouldn't have been a problem if I'd had my tools along, but who figured I'd need them?

Back down the fire escape. I paused at the fourth-floor landing, trying to decide if I wanted to take my chances with whoever was posted at ground level. I could always break into the basement and just hide there in the boiler room until the heat died down, but did I really want to do that? For that matter, did I want to scurry past the bedroom window of the Porlock apartment when the police were most likely already in there?

I took a moment to check the two fourth-floor apartments. The one on the right—4-D, I suppose, directly above the Porlock place—had its shade drawn. I pressed my ear to the windowpane and caught *Brady Bunch* reruns on the television set. The shade was drawn a few yards to the left at 4-C, but I couldn't hear anything inside, nor could I see any light around the edges of the window shade.

Of course the window was locked.

If I'd had a glass cutter I could have drawn a neat freehand circle on the appropriate pane of glass, reached in and turned the window lock. If I'd had some tape I could have broken any pane I wanted with no more noise than you'd make snapping a dry twig. If I'd had . . .

If wishes were horses, burglars would ride. I kicked in a pane of glass and closed my eyes until the tinkling stopped. I put my ear to the opening I'd created and listened for a moment or two, then unlocked the window, raised it, and stepped through it.

A few minutes later I left that apartment in a more conventional manner than I'd entered it, departing through the door and walking briskly down a flight of stairs. I encountered a couple of uniformed patrolmen on the third floor. The door to 3-D was open now, with other cops making themselves busy inside the apartment, while these two stood in the hall with nothing to do.

I asked one what the trouble was. He jutted out his chin at me and told me it was just routine. I nodded, reassured, and went down the other two flights and out.

I wanted to go home. It may or may not be where the heart is but it's where the burglar's tools are, and a burglar, like a workman, is only as good as his tools, and I felt naked without mine. I wasn't sure if the cops had a make on me yet. They'd get one before long, I was fairly sure of that, but I didn't doubt my ability to get in and out of my apartment before they set about looking for me. I had my tools there, I had cash there, and I would have liked to make a quick pit stop and equip myself for whatever lay ahead.

Because what lay ahead didn't look too good from where I sat. Madeleine Porlock had been left with more than the traditional number of holes in her head, and my fingerprints were undoubtedly plastered all over that apartment—on the cup I'd been drinking from, on the glass-topped table, and God knows where else. The same criminal genius that had wrapped my inert fingers around the murder gun would have seen to that.

The police would have a lot of questions for me, and they wouldn't even pay attention to my answers. I, on the other hand, had some hard questions of my own.

Who was Madeleine Porlock? How did she fit into the whole business? Why had she drugged me, and where had her killer come from, and why had he murdered her?

Whatever had become of Rudyard Whelkin?

And, finally, how did the Sikh fit into all of this?

The last question was no more easily answered than the others, but it made me realize I couldn't go home. By now the Sikh and whoever had sent him would know they'd been hoodwinked, which meant I had to avoid whatever places they might logically expect to find me. The store was out, obviously, and so was the apartment, since anyone with access to a Manhattan phone book can ferret out my address.

I flagged a cab heading downtown on Second Avenue. The driver was young and Hispanic, with alert eyes. Were those eyes registering me even as he asked my destination?

"The Village," I said.

"What part of it?"

"Sheridan Square."

He nodded shortly and away we went.

Carolyn Kaiser's apartment was on Arbor Court, one of those side-goggled Village lanes I can only find if I start out from the right place. Sheridan Square was the wrong place, so I had to walk up to Greenwich Avenue and then west and south until I hit it. I didn't remember which building was hers, so I went into the vestibules of several until I found her name on a mailbox and rang her bell.

Nobody home. I'd have called first but I didn't have her number with me and it was unlisted, and it's easier to pass a needle through the eye of a camel than to get an unlisted number out of an Information operator. It's hard enough to get listed numbers. I rang a couple of top-floor bells until someone buzzed me into the building. Carolyn lived on the first floor. I took one look at the locks on her door and turned around and left.

I checked a couple of hardware stores on Hudson. All closed. There was a locksmith, but could I really ask him to sell me burglar's tools? I didn't even try. I went to a drugstore and bought masking tape and paper clips and hairpins and a couple of nail files. At the tobacco counter I added a pipesmoker's gizmo equipped with different doo-hickeys for tamping, reaming, probing, and otherwise mistreating a pipe. It looked to be made of pretty decent steel.

I went back to Carolyn's building and annoyed the top-floor tenants again and got buzzed in a second time. I went to her door and got busy.

With my ring of picks and probes, the operation

wouldn't have taken five minutes. With makeshift tools
from the drugstore it took closer to ten, during which
time two persons entered the building and one left it. If
any of them took any notice of me they were too polite
to make a scene, and I finished the task at hand and let
myself into her place.

Cozy. Very Village, really. One room about fifteen
feet square with a teensy lavatory added on in back, so
small that your knees nudged the door when you sat on
the potty. The bathtub, a large claw-footed relic, was
over in the kitchen area with the sink and stove and
fridge; Carolyn had had a plywood cover cut to fit it so
that she could use it for chopping up vegetables. The
walls were painted blue, a deep rich tone, and the window frames and exposed plumbing were a bright yellow.

I used the loo, lit a fire under the leftover coffee (with
a match, the pilot didn't work), and let one of the cats
check me out. He was a Burmese and nothing intimi-
dated him. His buddy, a wary-eyed Russian Blue, reposed
on the double bed, where he tried to blend with the
patchwork quilt. I scratched the Burmese behind the ear
and he made that bizarre sound they make and rubbed
his head against my ankle. I guess I passed inspection.

The coffee boiled. I poured a cup, took a taste, and got
flashes of the mug of doctored coffee Madeleine Porlock
had given me. I poured it out, heated some water and
made some tea, and fortified the brew with an authorita-
tive slug of California brandy from a bottle I found on
the shelf over the sink.

It was six-thirty when I kept my appointment at
Chez Porlock, and I'd bolted from the place during the
seven o'clock newscast. I didn't look at my watch again
until I was sitting in Carolyn's wicker chair with my feet
up, the second cup of brandied tea half gone and the Rus-

sian Blue purring insanely in my lap. It was then just eighteen minutes after nine.

I moved the cat long enough to turn Carolyn's radio to one of the all-news stations, then settled back on the chair again. The cat reclaimed his place and helped me listen to a report on the Turkish earthquake and the presidential veto. There was a disgruntled Albanian holding a couple of people hostage up in Washington Heights, and a reporter on the scene did more than was necessary to put me right in the picture. I stroked the Russian Blue patiently while his Burmese buddy sat on top of a bookcase and made yowling noises.

It was coming up on eleven o'clock when I heard Carolyn's key in the lock. By then I'd switched to an FM jazz station and I had both cats on my lap. I stayed where I was while she unlocked the door, and as she opened it I said, "It's me, Carolyn. Don't panic."

"Why should I panic?" She came in, closed the door, locked up. "Been here long? I was over at the Duchess and you know what that's like. Except you probably don't, because they don't allow men in there." She slipped off her jacket, hung it on the doorknob, walked toward the coffeepot, then spun around suddenly and stared at me. "Hey," she said. "Did we make a date that I forgot?"

"No."

"Randy let you in? I thought she was visiting her goddam aunt in Bath Beach. What was she doing here? Did she go out to Brooklyn afterward or what?"

"I haven't seen Randy."

"Then how'd you get in, Bernie?"

"I sort of let myself in."

"Yeah, but where'd you get a key?" She frowned at me. Then light dawned. "Oh," she said, "*I* get it. Other people need keys. You're like Casper the Ghost. You walk through walls."

"Not exactly."

The cats had deserted my lap and were brushing themselves passionately against her ankles, desperate to be fed. She ignored them.

She said, "Bernie?"

"The radio."

"Huh?"

"It'll answer part of your question."

She listened, cocked her head. "Sounds like Monk," she said. "But I don't know, it's not as choppy as Monk and he's doing a lot of things with his left hand."

"It's Jimmy Rowles, but that's not what I meant. After the record ends, Carolyn."

After the record ended we got a quickie commercial for a jazz cruise to the Bahamas, and I had to explain that that wasn't it either. Then they gave us the eleven o'clock news, and high time, too. The Turkish earthquake, the flaky Albanian, the probable presidential veto, and then the extraordinary news that a convicted burglar, Bernard Rhodenbarr by name, was sought in connection with the murder of one Madeleine Porlock, who had been shot to death in her own apartment on East Sixty-sixth Street.

The announcer moved on to other matters. Carolyn cut him off in the middle of a sentence, looked at me for a moment, then went over to the kitchen area and fed the cats. "Chicken and kidneys tonight," she told them. "One of your all-time favorites, guys."

She stood for a moment with her back to me, her little hands on her hips, watching the wee rascals eat. Then she came over and sat on the edge of the bed.

"I should have known it was Jimmy Rowles," she

said. "I used to catch him at Bradley's all the time. I haven't been going there lately because Randy hates jazz, but if we break up, which I think we're in the process of doing, the hell, I'll get to the jazz clubs more, so it's an ill wind, right?"

"Right."

"Madeleine Doorlock? Funny name."

"Porlock."

"Still unusual. Who was she, Bern?"

"Beats me. We were strangers until this afternoon."

"You kill her?"

"No."

She crossed her legs at the knee, planted an elbow on the upper knee, cupped her hand, rested her chin in it. "All set," she announced. "You talk and I'll listen."

"Well," I said, "it's a long story."

NINE

I*T WAS* a long story, and she listened patiently through the whole thing, leaving the bed only to fetch the brandy bottle. When I finished she cracked the seal on a fresh bottle and poured us each a generous measure. I'd given up diluting mine with tea and she'd never started.

"Well, here's to crime," she said, holding her glass on high. "No wonder you almost spilled your club soda last time I said that. You were all set to go out and commit one. That's why you weren't drinking, huh?"

"I never drink when I work."

"I never work when I drink. Same principle. This is all taking me a little time to get used to, Bernie. I really believed you were a guy who used to be a burglar, but now you'd put all of that behind you and you were selling used books. Everything you told that policeman—"

"It was all true up to a point. I don't make a profit on the store, or maybe I do. I'm not much of an accountant. I buy and I sell, and I probably come out ahead, even allowing for rent and light bills and the phone and all. If I worked harder at it I could probably make enough to live on that way. If I hustled, and if I shelved paperbacks instead of wholesaling them, and if I read the want ads in *AB* every week and sent out price quotes all over the place."

"Instead you go out and knock off houses."

"Just once in a while."

"Special occasions."

"That's right."

"To make ends meet."

"Uh-huh."

She frowned in thought, scratched her head, sipped a little brandy. "Let's see," she said. "You came here because it's a safe place for you to be, right?"

"Right."

"Well, that's cool. We're friends, aren't we? I know it means I'm harboring a fugitive, and I don't particularly give a shit. What are friends for?"

"You're one in a million, Carolyn."

"You bet your ass. Listen, you can stay as long as you like and no questions asked, but the thing is I do have some questions, but I won't ask them if you don't want."

"Ask me anything."

"What's the capital of South Dakota? No, seriously, folks. Why'd you wait until the Arkwrights came home? Why not just duck in and out quick like a bunny? I always thought burglars preferred to avoid human contact."

I nodded. "It was Whelkin's idea. He wanted the book to be stolen without Arkwright even realizing it was gone. If I didn't take anything else and didn't disturb the house, and if the book was still there when Jesse Arkwright played his bedtime game of pocket billiards, it would be at least a day before he missed it. Whelkin was certain he'd be the prime suspect, because he wants the book so badly and he's had this feud with Arkwright, and an alibi wouldn't really help because Arkwright would just figure he hired someone to do it."

"Which he did do."

"Which he did do," I agreed. "But the longer it takes for Arkwright to know the book's missing, and the

harder it is for him to dope out how or when it disappeared, and the more time Whelkin has to tuck it away
where it will never be found—"

"And that's why you just took the book and left everything else."

"Right."

"Okay. That part makes sense now, I guess. But what
happened to Whelkin?"

"I don't know."

"You figure he killed her?"

"I don't think so."

"Why not? He set up the meeting. He got her to drug
you, and then when you were unconscious he killed
her."

"Why?"

"To frame you, I suppose. To get you out of the picture."

"Why not just kill me?"

"I don't know." She gnawed at a knuckle. "She can't
just come out of the air, this Porlock babe. Whelkin sent
you to her, she doped your coffee, and she must have
been after the book because she was asking you for it
before you had a chance to nod out. Then she frisked you
and took it herself."

"Or the killer did."

"You never heard a gunshot?"

"I was really out cold. And maybe he used a silencer,
but if he did he took it along with him. He also took the
book, plus the five hundred dollars the Sikh gave me." I
shrugged. "I figured all along that was too much to
charge for a reprint copy of *Soldiers Three*. Well, easy
come, easy go."

"That's what they say. Maybe the Sikh killed her."

"How do you figure that?"

"Maybe they were working together and he double-crossed her at the end." She shrugged elaborately. "I don't know, Bern. I'm just spinning my wheels a little. She must have been connected with Whelkin, though, don't you think?"

"I suppose so. He did lead me straight to her apartment. But—"

"But what?"

"But why wouldn't he just *buy* the book?"

"Maybe he couldn't afford it. But you're right, that would have been the easiest thing for him to do. He already paid you some of it in advance, didn't he? How much did he still owe you?"

I didn't say anything.

"Bernie?"

I sighed. "Just yesterday," I said, "I told a shoplifter he was too dumb to steal. He's not the only one."

"You didn't—"

"I didn't get *any* of the money in advance."

"Oh."

I shrugged, sighed, drank. "He was a member of the Martingale Club," I said. "Had a sort of English accent. Dressed very tweedy."

"So?"

"So his front snowed me, that's all. He finessed the whole topic of advance payment. I don't know how, but I walked into that house with nothing in my pocket but my hands. Jesus, Carolyn, I even dipped into my own funds for gasoline and bridge tolls. I'm beginning to feel really stupid."

"Whelkin conned you. He set you up and she polished you off, and then he shot her and left you in the frame."

I thought it over. "No," I said.

"No?"

"I don't think so. Why use her at all? He could slip me a mickey as easily as she could. And there's something else. That last telephone conversation I had with him, when he set up the meeting at her apartment. He sounded out of synch. I thought at the time he'd been drinking."

"So?"

"I bet they drugged him."

"The way they drugged you?"

"Not quite. Not the same drug, or the poor bastard wouldn't have been able to talk at all. I wonder what she gave me. It must have been powerful stuff. It had me hallucinating."

"Like acid?"

"I never had any acid."

"Neither did I."

"And this wasn't that kind of hallucination, with animals materializing on the walls and things like that. My perceptions just got distorted there before I blacked out. The music was getting loud and soft alternately, for example. And her face seemed to melt when I stared at it, but that was just before I went under."

"And you said something about her hair."

"Right, it kept turning orange. She had really short hair, dark brown, and I kept flashing that she had a head full of bright orange curls. Then I would blink and she'd have short dark hair again. Oh, for Christ's sake."

"What is it, Bernie?"

"I know where I saw her before. And she *did* have curly orange hair. It must have been a wig."

"The dark hair?"

"The orange hair. She came to the shop and she must have been wearing an orange wig. I'm positive it was the same woman. Squared shoulders, blocky figure, a kind of a stern square-jawed face—I'm positive it was her. She must have come to the shop three or four times."

"With Rudyard Whelkin?"

"No. He only came there once. Then we had lunch in the Martingale Club that same day, and I met him once more at the club for drinks and we talked several times over the phone. She came to the shop—well, I don't know when I first noticed her, but it must have been within the past week. Then yesterday she bought a book from me. Virgil's *Eclogues*, the Heritage Club edition. It was her. No question about it."

"What was she doing?"

"Looking things over, I suppose. Same reason I went out to Forest Hills with a clipboard. Reconnaissance. Say, can I put the radio on?"

"What for?"

"Midnight news."

"It's that time already? Sure, put it on."

I moved a cat and switched on the radio. I sat down and the cat returned to my lap and resumed purring. The news broadcast was a repeat of the eleven o'clock summary, except that the Albanian had surrendered without harming any of his hostages. He'd evidently gone bananas when he learned that his common-law wife had another common-law husband, which made them common-law husbands-in-law, or something. Madeleine Porlock was still dead and the police were still looking for one Bernard Rhodenbarr.

I moved the cat again, switched off the news, and sat down again. Carolyn asked me how it felt to be wanted by the police. I told her it felt terrible.

"How'd they know it was you, Bernie? Finger-prints?"

"Or the wallet."

"What wallet?"

"My wallet. Whoever frisked me got it—Madeleine Porlock or her killer. The book, the five hundred bucks, and the wallet. Maybe somebody stashed it where the cops would be sure to find it."

"Weren't you supposed to be unconscious when they arrived?"

"Maybe the wallet was a form of insurance. Or maybe the killer took the wallet on the chance I had something incriminating in it, like the card Whelkin gave me or some notes to myself." I shrugged. "I suppose the wallet could be anywhere right now. I suppose I should be all worked up about stopping my MasterCharge card before someone charges a ton of airline tickets to my account. Somehow that's way down on my list of priorities."

"I can understand that." She put her chin in her hand again and leaned forward to fasten her blue eyes on me. "What's at the top of the list, Bernie?"

"Huh?"

"The priority list. What are you going to do?"

"Beats me."

"How about another drink while you think about it?" I shook my head. "I think I've had enough."

"I had enough two or three drinks ago but I'm not going to let a little thing like that stop me." She got the bottle and helped herself. "You can just know when you've had enough and then stop?"

"Sure."

"That's remarkable," she said. She sipped her brandy, looked at me over the brim of the glass. "Did you know there was anybody else in the apartment? Besides the Porlock woman?"

"No. But I never got past the living room until she was dead. I thought it was just the two of us and we were waiting for Whelkin."

"The killer could have been in the other room."

"It's possible."

"Or she was alone, and she drugged you and took the book and the money and the wallet, and then she was on her way out the door and in came a man with a gun."

"Right."

"Who? The Sikh? Whelkin?"

"I dunno, Carolyn."

"Why on earth would she wear a wig? I mean, she wasn't anybody you knew to begin with, right? So why would she want to disguise herself?"

"Beats me."

"How about the Sikh? Was that a disguise? Maybe the Sikh was Rudyard Whelkin."

"He had a beard and a turban."

"The beard could have been a fake. And a turban is something you can put on and then take off."

"The Sikh was enormous. Six-four easy, maybe more."

"You never heard of elevator shoes?"

"Whelkin wasn't the Sikh," I said. "Trust me."

"All I do is trust you. But back to the other question. How do you get out of the mess you're in? Can you go to the cops?"

"That's the one thing I *can't* do. They'll book me for Murder One. I could try pleading to a lesser charge, or gamble that my lawyer could find a way to addle the jury, but the odds are I'd spend the next ten or twenty years with free room and board. I don't really want to do that."

"I can understand that. Jesus. Can't you—"

"Can't I what?"

"Tell them what you told me? Scratch that question, huh? Just blame it on the brandy. Because why on earth would they believe you? Nobody'd believe a story like yours except a dyke who shaves dogs. Bernie, there's got to be a way out, but what the hell is it?"

"Find the real killer."

"Oh, sure," she said. She clapped a hand to her forehead. "Now why didn't I think of that? Just find the real killer, solve the crime, get the stolen book back, and everything's copasetic. Just like TV, right? With everything wrapped up in time for the final commercial."

"And some scenes from next week's show," I said. "Don't forget that."

We talked for a while longer. Then Carolyn started yawning intermittently and I caught it from her. We agreed that we ought to get some sleep. We weren't accomplishing anything now and our minds were too tired to work properly.

"You'll stay here," she said. "You take the bed."

"Don't be silly. I'll take the couch."

"Don't *you* be silly. You're six feet long and so's the bed. I'm five feet long and so's the couch. It's good the Sikh didn't drop in because there's no place to put him."

"I just thought—"

"Uh-huh. The couch is perfectly comfortable and I sleep on it a lot. I wind up there whenever Randy and I have a medium-level fight."

"What's a medium-level fight?"

"The kind where she doesn't go home to her own apartment."

"I didn't know she had one. I thought the two of you lived together."

"We do, but she's got a place on Morton Street. Smaller than this, if you can believe it. Thank God she's got a place of her own, so that she can move right back into it when we split up."

"Maybe you should stay there tonight, Carolyn." She started to say something but I pressed onward. "If you're at her place, then you're not an accessory after the fact. But if you're here, then there's no question but that you're harboring a fugitive, and—"

"I'll take my chances, Bernie."

"Well—"

"Besides, it's possible Randy didn't go to Bath Beach. It's possible she's home."

"Couldn't you stay with her, anyway?"

"Not if someone else is staying with her at the same time."

"Oh."

"Uh-huh. We live in a world of infinite possibilities. You get the bed and I get the couch. Okay?"

"Okay."

I helped her make up the couch. She went into the lavatory and emerged wearing Dr. Denton's and scowling as if daring me to laugh. I did not laugh.

I washed up at the kitchen sink, turned off the light, stripped down to my underwear and got into bed. For a while nobody said anything.

Then she said, "Bern?"

"Yes?"

"I don't know how much you know about gay women, but you probably know that some of us are bisexual. Primarily gay but occasionally interested in going to bed with a man."

"Uh, I know."

"I'm not like that."

"I didn't think you were, Carolyn."

"I'm exclusively gay."

"That's what I figured."

"I figured it went without saying, but it's been my experience that a lot of things that go without saying, that you're better off if you say them."

"I understand."

More silence.

"Bernie? She took the five hundred dollars and the wallet, right?"

"I had about two hundred dollars in my wallet, too. That was an expensive cup of coffee she gave me, let me tell you."

"How'd you pay for the cab?"

"Huh?"

"The cab downtown. And how did you buy that stuff at the drugstore so you could pick my lock? What did you use for money?"

"Oh," I said.

"Do you keep a few extra dollars in your shoe for emergencies?"

"Well, no," I said. "Not that it doesn't sound like a good idea, but no, Carolyn."

"Well?"

"I told you about the fire escape, didn't I? How I tried the roof and that was no good, so I went down and broke into an apartment on the fourth floor?"

"You told me."

"Well, uh, since I was there and all, I, uh, took a few minutes to look around. Opened a few drawers."

"In the fourth-floor apartment?"

"That's right. There was just small change in a

dresser drawer, but one of the kitchen canisters had money in it. You'd be surprised how many people keep cash in the kitchen."

"And you took it?"

"Sure. I got a little over sixty dollars. Not enough to retire on, but it covered the cab and what I spent at the drugstore."

"Sixty dollars."

"More like sixty-five. Plus the bracelet."

"The bracelet?"

"Couldn't resist it," I said. "There was other jewelry that didn't tempt me at all, but this one bracelet—well, I'll show you in the morning."

"You'll show me in the morning."

"Sure. Don't let me forget."

"Jesus!"

"What's the matter?"

"You actually committed a burglary."

"Well, I'm a burglar, Carolyn."

"That's what I have to get used to. You're a burglar. You steal things out of people's homes. That's what burglars do. They steal things."

"As a general rule."

"You took the money because you needed it. Your own money was gone and you had to get away from the police and the money was there, so you took it."

"Right."

"And you took the bracelet because— Why'd you take the bracelet, Bernie?"

"Well—"

"Because it was there. Like Mt. Everest. But it was a bracelet instead of a mountain, and instead of climbing it you stole it."

"Carolyn—"

"It's all right, Bernie. Honest it is. I'll get used to it. You'll show me the bracelet in the morning?"

"I'll show you right now if you want."

"No, the morning's soon enough, Bernie. Bernie?"

"What?"

"Goodnight, Bernie."

"Goodnight, Carolyn."

TEN

I<small>T WAS ONE</small> of those chatty morning programs that tells you more about weather and traffic than anyone could possibly care to know. There was a massive tie-up on the Major Deegan Expressway, I learned, and a thirty percent chance of rain.

"Something ominous has happened to weather reports," I told Carolyn. "Have you noticed how they never tell you what it's going to do anymore? They just quote you the odds."

"I know."

"That way they're never wrong because they've never gone out on a limb. If they say there's a five percent chance of snow and we wind up hip-deep in it, all that means is a long shot came in. They've transformed the weather into some sort of celestial crap game."

"There's another muffin, Bernie."

"Thanks." I took it, buttered it. "It's all tied into the moral decline of the nation," I said. "Lottery tickets. Off-track betting. Gambling casinos in Atlantic City. Can you tell me what in the hell a thirty percent chance of rain means? What do I do, carry a third of an umbrella?"

"Here comes the news, Bernie."

I ate my muffin and sipped my coffee and listened to the news. My reaction to the weather report notwithstanding, I felt pretty good. My sleep had been deep and uninterrupted, and Carolyn's morning coffee, unadulterated with chicory or knockout drops, had my eyes all the way open.

So I sat wide-eyed and heard how I'd gained access to the house on Sixty-sixth Street via the fire escape, first visiting the fourth-floor apartment of Mr. and Mrs. Arthur Blinn, where I'd stolen an undisclosed sum of money, a diamond bracelet, a Piaget wristwatch, several miscellaneous pieces of jewelry, and a full-length Russian sable coat. I'd descended a flight to 3-D, where Madeleine Porlock had interrupted my larcenous labors, only to be shot dead with a .32-caliber automatic for her troubles. I'd left the gun behind, escaping with my loot, scampering down the fire escape moments before the police arrived on the scene.

When the announcer moved on to other topics I switched him off. Carolyn had a funny expression on her face. I reached into my pants pocket and came up with the bracelet, plopping it down on the table in front of her. She turned it in her hand so that light glinted off the stones.

"Pretty," she said. "What's it worth?"

"I could probably get a few hundred for it. Art Deco's the rage these days. But I just took it because I liked the looks of it."

"Uh-huh. What did the coat look like?"

"I never even looked in the closets. Oh, you thought—" I shook my head. "More evidence of the moral decline of the nation," I said. "All I took was the cash and the bracelet, Carolyn. The rest was a little insurance scam the Blinns decided to work."

"You mean—"

"I mean they decided they've been paying premiums all these years, so why not take advantage of the burglary they've been waiting for? A coat, a watch, some miscellaneous jewelry, and of course they'll report a higher cash loss than they actually sustained, and even if the insurance company chisels a little, they'll wind up four or five grand to the good."

"Jesus," she said. "Everybody's a crook."

"Not quite," I said. "But sometimes it seems that way."

⋘⟳⋙

I made up the bed while she did up the breakfast dishes. Then we sat down with the last of the coffee and tried to figure out where to start. There seemed to be two loose ends we could pick at, Madeleine Porlock and J. Rudyard Whelkin.

"If we knew where he was," I said, "we might be able to get somewhere."

"We already know where *she* is."

"But we don't know who she is. Or was. I wish I had my wallet. I had his card. His address was somewhere in the East Thirties but I don't remember the street or the number."

"That makes it tough."

"You'd think I'd remember the phone number. I dialed it enough yesterday." I picked up the phone, dialed the first three numbers hoping the rest would come to me, then gave up and cradled the phone. The phone book didn't have him and neither did the Information operator. There was an M. Porlock in the book, though, and for no particular reason I dialed the listed number. It rang a few times and I hung up.

"Maybe we should start with the Sikh," Carolyn suggested.

"We don't even know his name."

"That's a point."

"There ought to be something about her in the paper. The radio just gives you the surface stuff, but there ought to be something beyond that in the *Times*. Where she worked and if she was married, that kind of thing."

"And Whelkin belonged to the Martingale Club."

"True."

"So we've each got a place to start, Bernie. I'll be back in a minute." It was closer to ten minutes when she returned with both papers. She read the *News* while I read the *Times*. Then we switched.

"Not a whole lot," I said.

"Something, though. Who do you want, Whelkin or Porlock?"

"Don't you have to trim a poodle or something?"

"I'm taking Whelkin. You've got Porlock, Bernie. Okay?"

"Okay."

"I guess I'll go over to his club. Maybe I can learn something that way."

"Maybe."

"How about you? You won't leave the apartment, will you?"

I shook my head. "I'll see what I can find out over the phone."

"That sounds like a good idea."

"And maybe I'll pray a little."

"To whom? St. Dismas?"

"Wouldn't hurt."

"Or the lost-objects guy, because we ought to see about getting that book back."

"Anthony of Padua."

"Right."

"Actually," I said, "I was thinking more of St. Raymond Nonnatus. Patron saint of the falsely accused."

She looked at me. "You're making this up."

"That's a false accusation, Carolyn."

"You're not making it up?"

"Nope."

"There's really a—"

"Yep."

"Well, by all means," she said. "Pray."

ᘒᕯᘒ

The phone started ringing minutes after she left the apartment. It rang five times and stopped. I picked up the *Times* and it started ringing again and rang twelve times before it quit. I read somewhere that it only takes a minute for a telephone to ring twelve times. I'll tell you, it certainly seemed longer than that.

I went back to the *Times*. The back-page story gave Madeleine Porlock's age as forty-two and described her as a psychotherapist. The *Daily News* had given her age but didn't tell what she did for a living. I tried to imagine her with a note pad and a faint Viennese accent, asking me about my dreams. Had she had an office elsewhere? The Victorian love seat was a far cry from the traditional analyst's couch.

Maybe Whelkin was her patient. He told her all about his scheme to gain possession of *The Deliverance of Fort Bucklow*, and then she hypnotized him and got him to make the call to me, and then he got unhypnotized and killed her and took the book back, and . . .

I called the *Times*, got through to someone in the city room. I explained I was Art Matlovich of the Cleveland *Plain Dealer*. We thought the Porlock woman might be a former resident of Cleveland, and did they have anything on her besides what they'd run in the paper?

What they had was mostly negative. No information about next of kin. No clue as to where she'd lived before taking the Sixty-sixth Street apartment fourteen months ago. If she'd ever been in Cleveland, or even flown over the State of Ohio, they didn't know anything about it.

The same call to the *News* was about as unproductive. The man I talked to said he didn't know where the *Times* got off calling Porlock a psychotherapist, that he had the impression she was somebody's mistress, but that they weren't really digging into it because all she was was the victim of an open-and-shut burglary turned homicide. "It's not much of a story for us," he said. "Only reason we played it at all is it's the Upper East Side. See, that's a posh neighborhood and all. I don't know what the equivalent would be in Cleveland."

Neither did I, so I let it pass.

"This Rhodenbarr," the *News* man went on. "They'll pick him up tomorrow or the next day and that's the end of the story. No sex angle, nothing colorful like that. He's just a burglar."

"Just a burglar," I echoed.

"Only this time he killed somebody. They'll throw the key away on him this time. He's a guy had his name in the papers before. In connection with homicide committed during a job he was pulling. Up to now he always managed to weasel out of it, but this time he's got his dick in the wringer."

"Don't be too sure of that," I said.

"Huh?"

"I mean you never know," I said quickly. "The way criminals manage to slip through cracks in the criminal-justice apparatus these days."

"Jesus," he said. "You sound like you been writin' our editorials."

I no sooner hung up the phone than it started ringing. I put up a fresh pot of coffee. The phone stopped ringing. I went over to it, about to make a call, and it rang again. I waited it out, then used it to call the police. This time I said I was Phil Urbanik of the Minneapolis *Tribune*. I was tired of Cleveland for the time being. I got bounced from one cop to another, spending a lot of time on Hold in the process, before I managed to establish that nobody around the squadroom knew more about Madeleine Porlock than that she was dead. The last cop I spoke with was sure of one other thing, too.

"No question," he said. "Rhodenbarr killed her. One bullet, close range, smack in the forehead. M.E.'s report says death was instantaneous, which you don't have to be a doctor to tell. He left prints in both apartments."

"He must have been careless," I suggested.

"Getting old and sloppy. Losing his touch. Here's a guy, his usual M.O.'s to wear rubber gloves with the palms cut out so he don't leave a print anywhere."

"You know him?"

"No, but I seen his sheet. You'd figure him to be pretty slick, plus he always stayed away from violence, and here he's sloppy enough to leave prints and he went and killed a woman. You know what I figure? What I figure is drugs."

"He's involved with drugs?"

"I think he musta been high on them. You get hopped up and you're capable of anything."

"How about the gun? Was it his?"

"Maybe he found it there. We didn't trace it yet. Could be the Porlock woman had it for protection. It wasn't registered, but what does that mean? Maybe he stole it upstairs. The couple up there said no, but if it was an unregistered weapon they'd deny it. What's your interest in the gun, anyway?"

"Just making conversation."

"Minneapolis, you said?"

"That's right," I said smoothly. "Well, I guess that gives us a good hometown angle on the story. All right to say you're close to an arrest?"

"Oh, we'll get him," he assured me. "A crook like Rhodenbarr's a creature of habit. He'll be what they call frequenting his old haunts and we'll pick him up. Just a question of time."

᠁᠁᠁

I was standing behind the door when she opened it. She moved into the room saying my name.

"Behind you," I said, as gently as possible. She clapped her hand to her chest as if to keep her heart where it belonged.

"Jesus," she said. "Don't *do* that."

"Sorry. I wasn't sure it was you."

"Who else would it be?"

"It could have been Randy."

"Randy," she said heavily. Cats appeared and threaded figure eights around her ankles. "Randy. I don't suppose she called, did she?"

"She might have. It rang a lot but I wasn't answering it."

"I know you weren't. I called twice myself, and when you didn't answer I figured you weren't picking up the phone, but I also figured maybe you got cabin fever and went out, and then I came home and you weren't here and all of a sudden you were behind me. Don't do that again, huh?"

"I won't."

"I had a busy day. What time is it? Almost two? I've been running all over the place. I found out some stuff. What's this?"

"I want you to make a phone call for me."

She took the sheet of paper I handed her but looked at me instead. "Don't you want to hear what I found out?"

"In a minute. I want you to call the *Times* and insert the ad before they close."

"What ad?"

"The one I just handed you. In the Personal column."

"You got some handwriting. You should have been a doctor, did anyone ever tell you that? 'Space available on Kipling Society charter excursion to Fort Bucklow. Interested parties call 989–5440.' That's my number."

"No kidding."

"You're going to put my number in the paper?"

"Why not?"

"Somebody'll read it and come here."

"How? By crawling through the wires? The phone's unlisted."

"No, it's not. This place is a sublet, Bernie, so I kept the phone listed under Nathan Aranow. He's the guy I sublet from. It's like having an unlisted number except there's no extra charge for the privilege, and whenever I get a call for a Nathan Aranow I know it's some pest trying to sell me a subscription to something I don't want. But it's a listed number."

"So?"

"So the address is in the book. Nathan Aranow, 64 Arbor Court, and the telephone number."

"So somebody could read the ad and then just go all

the way through the phone book reading numbers until they came to this one, right, Carolyn?"

"Oh. You can't get the address from the number?"

"No."

"Oh. I hope nobody does go through the book, because Aranow's right in the front."

"Maybe they'll start in the back."

"I hope so. This ad—"

"A lot of people seem to be anxious to get their hands on this book," I explained. "All different people, the way it looks to me. And only one of them knows I don't have it. So if I give the impression that I do have it, maybe one or more of them will get in touch and I'll be able to figure out what's going on."

"Makes sense. Why didn't you just place the ad yourself? Afraid somebody in the *Times* classified department would recognize your voice?"

"No."

"And they'd say, 'Aha, it's Bernard G. Rhodenbarr the burglar, and let's go through the telephone wires and take him into custody.' My God, Bernie, you thought I was being paranoid about the number, and you're afraid to make a phone call."

"They call back," I said.

"Huh?"

"When you place an ad with a phone number. To make sure it's not a practical joke. And the phone was ringing constantly, and I wasn't answering it, and I figured the *Times* would call to confirm the ad and how would I know it was them? Paranoia, I suppose, but it seemed easier to wait and let *you* make the call, although I'm beginning to wonder. You'll place the ad for me, won't you?"

"Sure," she said, and the phone rang as she was reaching for it.

She picked it up, said, "Hello?" Then she said, "Listen, I can't talk to you right now. Where are you and I'll call you back." Pause. "Company? No, of course not." Pause. "I was at the shop. Oh. Well, I was in and out all day. One thing after another." Pause. "Dammit, I *can't* talk now, and—" She took the receiver from her ear and looked beseechingly at me. "She hung up," she said.

"Randy?"

"Who else? She thought I had company."

"You do."

"Yeah, but she thought you were a woman."

"Must be my high-pitched voice."

"What do you mean? You didn't say anything. Oh, I see. It's a joke."

"It was trying to be one."

"Yeah, right." She looked at the telephone receiver, shook her head at it, hung it up. "She called here all morning," she said. "And called the store, too, and I was out, obviously, and now she thinks—" The corners of her mouth curled slowly into a wide grin. "How about that?" she said. "The bitch is jealous."

"Is that good?"

"It's terrific." The phone rang again, and it was Randy. I tried not to pay too much attention to the conversation. It ended with Carolyn saying, "Oh, you demand to know who I've got over here? All right, I'll tell you who I've got over here. I've got my aunt from Bath Beach over here. You think you're the only woman in Manhattan with a mythical aunt in Bath Beach?"

She hung up, positively radiant. "Gimme the ad," she said. "Quick, before she calls back. You wouldn't believe how jealous she is."

She got the ad in, then answered the phone when they called back to confirm it. Then she was getting lunch on the table, setting out bread and cheese and opening a couple bottles of Amstel, when the phone rang again. "Randy," she said. "I'm not getting it."

"Fine."

"You had this all morning, huh? The phone ringing like that?"

"Maybe eight, ten times. That's all."

"You find out anything about Madeleine Porlock?"

I told her about the calls I'd made.

"Not much," she said.

"Next to nothing."

"I learned a little about your friend Whelkin, but I don't know what good it does. He's not a member of the Martingale Club."

"Don't be silly. I ate there with him."

"Uh-huh. The Martingale Club of New York maintains what they call reciprocity with a London club called Poindexter's. Ever hear of it?"

"No."

"Me neither. The dude at the Martingale said it as though it was a household word. The Martingale has reciprocity with three London clubs, he told me. White's, Poindexter's, and the Dolphin. I never heard of any of them."

"I think I heard of White's."

"Anyhow, that's how Whelkin got guest privileges. But I thought he was an American."

"I think he is. He has an accent that could be English, but I figured it was an affectation. Something he picked up at prep school, maybe." I thought back to conversations we'd had. "No," I said, "he's American. He talked about making a trip to London to attend that auction, and he referred to the English once as 'our cousins across the pond.' "

"Honestly?"

"Honestly. I suppose he could be an American and belong to a London club, and use that London membership to claim guest privileges at the Martingale. I suppose it's possible."

"Lots of things are possible."

"Uh-huh. You know what I think?"

"He's a phony."

"He's a phony who faked me out of my socks, that's what he is. God, the more I think about it the phonier he sounds, and I let him con me into stealing the book with no money in front. All of a sudden his whole story is starting to come apart in my hands. All that happy horseshit about Haggard and Kipling, all that verse he quoted at me."

"You think he just made it all up?"

"No, but—"

"Leave me alone, Ubi. You don't even like Jarlsberg." Ubi was short for Ubiquitous, which was the Russian Blue's name. Jarlsberg was the cheese we were munching. (Not the Burmese, in case you were wondering. The Burmese was named Archie.)

To me she said, "Maybe the book doesn't exist, Bernie."

"I had it in my hands, Carolyn."

"Oh, right."

"I was thinking that myself earlier, just spinning all sorts of mental wheels. Like it wasn't a real book, it was hollowed out and all full of heroin or something like that."

"Yeah, that's an idea."

"Except it's a dumb idea, because I actually flipped

through that book and read bits and pieces of it, and it's real. It's a genuine old printed book in less than sensational condition. I was even wondering if it could be a fake."

"A fake?"

"Sure. Suppose Kipling destroyed every last copy of *The Deliverance of Fort Bucklow*. Suppose there never was such a thing as a Rider Haggard copy to survive, or suppose there was but it disappeared forever." She was nodding encouragingly. "Well," I went on, "suppose someone sat down and faked a text. It'd be a job, writing that long a ballad, but Kipling's not the hardest writer in the world to imitate. Some poet could knock it out between greeting-card assignments."

"Then what?"

"Well, you couldn't sell it as an original manuscript because it would be too easily discredited. But if you had a printer set type—" I shook my head. "That's where it breaks down. You could set type and run off one copy, and you could bind it and then distress it one way or another to give it some age, and you could even fake the inscription to H. Rider Haggard in a way that might pass inspection. But do you see the problem?"

"It sounds complicated."

"Right. It's too damned complicated and far too expensive. It's like those caper movies where the crooks would have had to spend a million dollars to steal a hundred thousand, with all the elaborate preparations they go through and the equipment they use. Any crook who went through everything I described in order to produce a book you could sell for fifteen thousand dollars would have to be crazy."

"Maybe it's worth a lot more than that. Fifteen thousand is just the price you and Whelkin worked out."

"That's true. The fifteen-thousand figure doesn't really mean anything, since I didn't even get a smell of it, did I?" I sighed. Wistfully, I imagine. "No," I said. "I know an old book when I look at it. I look at a few thousand of them every day, and old books are different from new ones, dammit. Paper's different when it's been around for fifty years. Sure, they could have used old paper, but it keeps not being worth the trouble. It's a real book, Carolyn. I'm sure of it."

"Speaking of the old books you look at every day."

"What about them?"

"Somebody's watching your store. I was at my shop part of the time, I had to wash a dog and I couldn't reach the owner to cancel. And there was somebody in a car across the street from your shop, and he was still there when I walked past a second time."

"Did you get a good look at him?"

"No. I didn't get the license number, either. I suppose I should have, huh?"

"What for?"

"I don't know."

"It was probably the police," I said. "A stakeout."

"Oh."

"They've probably got my apartment staked out, too."

"Oh. That's how they do it, huh?"

"That's how they do it on television. This cop I talked to earlier said they'd get me when I returned to my old haunts. I wanted to tell him I didn't have any old haunts, but I suppose he meant the store and the apartment."

"Or this place."

"Huh?"

"Well, we're friends. You come over here a lot. If they talk to enough people they'll learn that, won't they?"

"I hope not," I said, and the phone rang. We looked at each other, not very happily, and didn't say a word until it stopped ringing.

ELEVEN

At six-fifteen I was sitting at the counter of the Red Flame at the corner of Seventieth and West End. I had a cup of coffee and a wedge of prune Danish in front of me and I wasn't particularly interested in either. The other two customers, a teenaged couple in a back booth, were interested only in each other. The counterman wasn't interested in anything; he stood beside the coffee urns chewing a mint-flavored toothpick and staring at the opposite wall, where a bas-relief showed a couple of olive-skinned youths chasing sheep over a Greek hillside. He shook his head from time to time, evidently wondering what the hell he was doing here.

I kept glancing out the window and wondering much the same thing. From where I sat I could almost see my building a block uptown. I'd had a closer look earlier from the sidewalk, but I hadn't been close enough then to tell if there were cops staked out in or around the place. Theoretically it shouldn't matter, but theoretically bumblebees can't fly, so how much faith can you place in theory?

One of the teenagers giggled. The counterman yawned and scratched himself. I looked out the window for perhaps the forty-first time and saw Carolyn half a block away, heading south on West End with my small suitcase in one hand. I put some money on the counter and went out to meet her.

She was radiant. "Piece of cake," she said. "Nothing to it, Bern. This burglary number's a cinch."

"Well, you had my keys, Carolyn."

"They helped, no question about it. Of course, I had to get the right key in the right lock."

"You didn't have any trouble getting into the building?"

She shook her head. "Mrs. Hesch was terrific. The doorman called her on the intercom and she said to send me right up, and then she met me at the elevator."

I'd called Mrs. Hesch earlier to arrange all this. She was a widow who had the apartment across the hall from me, and she seemed to think burglary was the sort of character defect that could be overlooked in a friend and neighbor.

"She didn't have to meet you," I said.

"Well, she wanted to make sure I found the right apartment. What she really wanted was a good look at me. She's a little worried about you, Bern."

"Hell, I'm a little worried about me myself."

"She thought you were all respectable now, what with the bookstore and all. Then she heard about the Porlock murder on the news last night and she started to worry. But she's positive you didn't kill anybody."

"Good for her."

"I think she liked me. She wanted me to come in for coffee but I told her there wasn't time."

"She makes good coffee."

"That's what she said. She said you like her coffee a lot, and she sort of implied that what you need is somebody to make coffee for you on a full-time basis. The message I got is that living on the West Side and burgling on the East Side is a sort of Robin Hood thing, but there's a time in life when a young man should think about getting married and settling down."

"It's nice the two of you hit it off."

"Well, we only talked for a couple of minutes. Then I went and burgled your apartment." She hefted the suitcase. "I think I got everything. Burglar tools, pocket flashlight, all the things you mentioned. And shirts and socks and underwear. There was some cash in your shirt drawer."

"There was? I guess there was. I usually keep a few dollars there."

"Thirty-eight dollars."

"If you say so."

"I took it."

"Oh," I said. "Well, I don't suppose thirty-eight dollars one way or the other is going to make a difference. But it can't hurt to have it along."

She shrugged. "You said you always take cash," she said. "So I took it."

"It's a good principle. You know something? We're never going to get a cab."

"Not when it's raining. Can we get a subway? No, not across town. Isn't there a bus that goes over Seventy-ninth Street?"

"It's not a good idea to take buses when you're wanted for homicide. It's awfully public."

"I suppose we'll get a cab sooner or later."

I took the suitcase in one hand and her arm in the other. "The hell with that," I said. "We'll take a car."

The Pontiac was right where I'd left it. Sometimes the tow-truck division lets things slide for a while, and this time the Pontiac's owner was the beneficiary of their lapse. I popped the door on the passenger's side, let Carolyn in, and took a ticket from underneath the windshield wiper while she leaned across the seat to unlatch the door for me.

"See?" someone said. "You got a ticket. Did I tell you you'd get a ticket?"

I didn't recognize the man at first. Then I saw the brindle boxer at the end of the leash he was holding.

"Sooner or later," he told me, "they'll tow you away. Then what will you do?"

"Get another car," I said.

He shook his head, tugged impatiently at the dog's leash. "Come on, Max," he said. "Some people, you can't tell them a thing."

I got into the car, set about jumping the ignition. Carolyn watched the process, fascinated, and it wasn't until we pulled away from the curb that she asked who the man was and what he had wanted.

"He wanted to be helpful," I said, "but all in all he's a pest. The dog's all right, though. His name is Max. The dog, I mean."

"He looks okay," she said, "but he'd probably be murder to wash."

⁂

I left the Pontiac in a bus stop around the corner from where we were going. Carolyn said it might get towed and I said I didn't care if it did. I got tools and accessories from the suitcase, then left the case and the clothes it contained on the back seat of the Pontiac.

"Suppose they tow the car," she said, "and suppose

they identify the clothing from laundry marks. Then they'll know you were here, and—"

"You've been watching too much television," I said. "When they tow cars they take them over to that pier on the Hudson and wait for the owner to turn up. They don't check the contents. You could have a dead body in the trunk and they'd never know."

"I wish you hadn't said that," she said.

"There's nothing in the trunk."

"How do you know for sure?"

We went around the corner. No one seemed to be keeping an eye on the elegant little brownstone. A woman stood in the bay window on the parlor floor, watering the plants with a long-spouted watering can. The can was gleaming copper, the plants were all a lush green, and the whole scene was one of upper-middle-class domestic tranquillity. Outside, watching this and getting rained on, I felt like a street urchin in a Victorian novel.

I looked up. There were lighted windows on the third and fourth floors, but they didn't tell me anything. The apartments that interested me were at the rear of the building.

We entered the vestibule. "You don't have to come," I said.

"Ring the bell, Bern."

"I'm serious. You could wait in the car."

"Wonderful. I can play it safe by sitting in a stolen car parked at a bus stop. Why don't I just wait in the subway? I could cling to the third rail for security."

"What you could do is spend the next half-hour in the bar on the corner. Suppose we walk into an apartment full of cops?"

"Ring the bell, Bernie."

"It's just that I hate to see you walk into trouble."

"So do I, but let's play the hand out as dealt, huh? I'll be with the two of them so they can't get cute while you're downstairs. We worked it out before, Bern, and it made sense then and it still makes sense now. You want to know something? It's probably dangerous for us to spend the next six hours arguing in the vestibule, if you're so concerned with what's dangerous and what's not, so why don't you ring their bell and get it over with?"

First, though, I rang the bell marked *Porlock*. I poked it three times, waited half a minute, then gave it another healthy tickle. I didn't really expect a response and I was happy not to get one. My finger moved from the *Porlock* bell to the one marked *Blinn*. I gave it a long and two shorts, and the answering buzzer sounded almost at once. I pushed the door and it opened.

"Darn," Carolyn said. I looked at her. "Well, I thought I'd get to watch you pick it," she said. "That's all."

We went up the stairs and stopped at the third floor long enough to peek at the door of 3-D. As I'd figured it, the cops had sealed it, and the door was really plastered with official-looking material. I could have opened it with a scout knife, but I couldn't have done so without destroying the seals and making it obvious that I'd been there.

Instead, we went up another flight. The door of 4-C was closed. Carolyn and I looked at each other. Then I reached out a hand and knocked.

The door opened. Arthur Blinn stood with one hand on its knob and the other motioning us in. "Come on, come on," he said urgently. "Don't stand out there all night." In his hurry to close the door he almost hit Carolyn with it, but he got it shut and fussed with the locks and bolts. "You can relax now, Gert," he called out. "It's only the burglar."

They made a cute couple. They were both about five-six, both as roly-poly as panda bears. Both had curly dark-brown hair, although he'd lost most of his in the front. She was wearing a forest-green pants suit in basic polyester. He wore the trousers and vest of a gray glen-plaid business suit. His white shirt was unbuttoned at the neck and his tie was loosened for comfort. She poured coffee and pushed Scottish shortbread at us. He told us, over and over again, what a relief it was to see us.

"Because I told Gert, suppose it's a setup? Suppose it's the insurance company running a bluff? Because honestly, Mr. Rhodenbarr, who ever heard of such a thing? A burglar calls up, says hello, I'm you're friendly neighborhood burglar, and if you cooperate with me a little I won't rat to the insurance people and tell them your claim is lousy. I figured a burglar with troubles like you got, wanted for killing a woman and God knows what else, I figured you're not going to knock yourself out shouting you never stole a coat or a watch."

"And what *I* figured," Gert said, "is why would you be coming here, anyway? 'He wants to get rid of witnesses,' I told Artie. 'Remember, he already killed once.' "

"What I said is what did we ever witness? I told her, I said forget all that. Just hope it's the burglar, I told her. All we need is some insurance snoop. You don't care for the shortbread, young lady?"

"It's delicious," Carolyn said. "And Bernie never killed anybody, Mrs. Blinn."

"Call me Gert, honey."

"He never killed anyone, Gert."

"I'm sure of it, honey. Meeting him, seeing the two of you, my mind's a hundred percent at ease."

"He was framed, Gert. That's why we're here. To find out who really killed Madeleine Porlock."

"If we knew," Arthur Blinn said, "believe me, we'd tell you. But what do we know?"

"You lived in the same building with her. You must have known something about her."

The Blinns looked at each other and gave simultaneous little shrugs. "She wasn't directly under us," Gert explained. "So we wouldn't know if she had loud parties or played music all night or anything like that."

"Like Mr. Mboka," Artie said.

"In 3-C," Gert said. "He's African, you see, and he works at the U.N. Somebody said he was a translator."

"Plays the drums," Artie said.

"We don't know that, Artie. He either plays the drums or he plays recordings of drums."

"Same difference."

"But we haven't spoken to him about it because we thought it might be religious and we didn't want to interfere."

"Plus Gert here thinks he's a cannibal and she's *afraid* to speak to him."

"I don't think he's a cannibal," Gert protested. "Who ever said I thought he was a cannibal?"

I cleared my throat. "Maybe the two of you could talk to Carolyn about Miss Porlock," I suggested. "And if I could, uh, be excused for a few moments."

"You want to use the bathroom?"

"The fire escape."

Blinn furrowed his brow at me, then relaxed his features and nodded energetically. "Oh, right," he said. "For a minute there I thought— But to hell with what I thought. The fire escape. Sure. Right through to the bedroom. But you know the way, don't you? You were here yesterday. It's spooky, you know? The idea of someone else being in your apartment. Of course, it's not so spooky now that we know you, you and Carolyn here. But when we first found out about it, well, you can imagine."

"It must have been upsetting."

"That's exactly what it was. Upsetting. Gert called the super about the pane of glass, but it's like pulling teeth to get him to do anything around here. Generally he gets more responsive right before Christmas, so maybe we'll get some action soon. Meanwhile I taped up a shirt cardboard so the wind and rain won't come in."

"I'm sorry I had to break the window."

"Listen, these things happen."

I unlocked the window, raised it, stepped out onto the fire escape. The rain had stepped up a little and it was cold and windy out there. Behind me, Blinn drew the window shut again. He was reaching to lock it when I extended a finger and tapped on the glass. He caught himself, left the window unlocked, and smiled and shook his head at his absentmindedness. He went off chuckling to himself while I headed down a flight of steel steps.

This time I was properly equipped. I had my glass cutter and a roll of adhesive tape, and I used them to remove a pane from the Porlock window swiftly and silently. I turned the catch, raised the window, and let myself in.

"That's what I was talking about before," Gert said. "Listen. Can you hear it?"

"The drumming."

She nodded. "That's Mboka. Now, is that him drumming or is it a record? Because I can't tell."

"He was doing it while you were downstairs," Carolyn said. "Personally I think it's him drumming."

I said I couldn't tell, and that I'd been unable to hear him from the Porlock apartment.

"You never hear anything through the walls," Artie said. "Just through the floors and ceilings. It's a solid building as far as the walls are concerned."

"I don't mind the drumming most of the time," Gert said. "I'll play music and the drumming sort of fits in with it. It's in the middle of the night that it gets me, but I don't like to complain."

"She figures it's the middle of the afternoon in Africa."

We had a hard time getting out of there. They kept giving us shortbread and coffee and asking sincere little questions about the ins and outs of burglary. Finally we managed to fight our way to the door. We said our good-byes all around, and then Gert hung back a little while Artie caught my sleeve in the doorway.

"Say, Bernie," he said, "we all squared away now?"

"Sure thing, Artie."

"As far as the insurance company's concerned . . ."

"Don't worry about a thing. The coat, the watch, the other stuff. I'll back your claim."

"That's a relief," he said. "I must have been crazy, putting in that claim, but I'd look like a horse's ass changing it now, and why did we pay premiums all those years anyway, right?"

"Right, Artie."

"The thing is, I hate to mention this, but while you were downstairs Gert was wondering about the bracelet."

"How's that, Artie?"

"The bracelet you took. It was Gert's. I don't think it's worth much."

"A couple of hundred."

"That much? I would have said less. It belonged to her mother. The thing is, I wondered what's the chance of getting it back?"

"Oh," I said. "I see what you mean. Well, Artie, I'm kind of pressed right now."

"I can imagine."

"But when things are back to normal, I'm sure we can work something out."

He clapped me on the shoulder. "That's terrific," he said. "Listen, take all the time you need. There's no rush."

TWELVE

The Pontiac, untowed and unticketed, waited for us at the bus stop. The suitcase huddled undisturbed on the floor in back. All of this surprised Carolyn, but I'd expected nothing less. There was something about that car that inspired confidence.

On the way downtown I learned what Gert Blinn had told her. While I was a floor below in Madeleine Porlock's apartment, Gert had maneuvered Carolyn into the kitchen, presumably to copy down a recipe but actually to dish a little dirt. The late Madeleine Porlock, she'd confided, was no better than she should be.

"Gert was vague," Carolyn said. "I don't know that Porlock was a hooker exactly, but I got the impression that her life tended to revolve around men. Whenever Gert met her on the stairs she was with some man or other, and I gather that's how her rent got paid."

"Doesn't surprise me."

"Well, it surprises me," she said. "I never saw Porlock, but the way you described her she was the furthest thing from slinky. The woman you were talking about sounded like she could play the mean matron in all the old prison movies."

"That's on a bad day. On a good day she could have played the nurse in *Cuckoo's Nest.*"

"Uh-huh. Bern, I admit I don't know what men go

for, because it's never been a burning issue with me, but she doesn't sound the type to get her rent paid."

"You didn't go through her drawers and closets."

"Oh?"

A cab stopped abruptly in front of us. I swung the wheel to the right and slipped neatly around it. No question, I thought. The Pontiac and I were made for each other.

"Lots of sexy underwear," I said.

"Oh?"

"Wispy things. Scarlet gauze and black lace. Peekaboo bras."

"Men really go for that crap, huh?"

"So it would seem. Then there were a few garter belts, and a couple of tight corsets that you'd have to be a graduate engineer to figure out."

"Tight corsets?"

"A couple of pairs of boots with six-inch stiletto heels. Lots of leather stuff, including those cunning wrist and ankle bracelets decorated with metal studs."

"A subtle pattern begins to emerge."

"Doesn't it? And I haven't even mentioned the small but tasteful wardrobe in skintight black latex or the nifty collection of whips and chains. Or the whole dresser drawer full of gadgets which we might euphemistically designate as marital aids."

She twirled an imaginary mustache. "This Porlock creature," she said, "was into kink."

"A veritable mistress of kink," I said. "It was beginning to get to me, prowling around in all that weirdness."

"I'm surprised it didn't make the papers. *'Dominatrix Slain in East Side Pleasure Pad'*—that should be good for page three in the *Daily News* any day of the week."

"I thought of that. But nothing was out in plain sight, Carolyn, and when I was up there the first time, all I saw was a tastefully decorated apartment. Remember, the cops had an open-and-shut case, a woman shot in her own apartment by a burglar she'd evidently caught in the act. They didn't have any reason to toss her apartment. And she really lived there, it wasn't just her office. She had street clothes there, too, and there were dishes in the kitchen cupboards and Q-tips and dental floss in the medicine cabinet."

"Find any cash? Any jewelry?"

"There's a jar in the kitchen where she used to throw her pennies. And there was some loose jewelry in one of the bedroom drawers, but none of it looked like much. I didn't steal anything, if that's what you were getting at."

"I just wondered."

A siren opened up behind us. I edged over to the right to give them room. A blue-and-white police cruiser sailed past us, wailing madly, barreling on through a red light. I braked for the same light, and as we waited for it to turn green a pair of foot patrolmen crossed the street in front of us. The one with the mustache was doing baton-twirler tricks with his nightstick. At one point he swung around so that he was looking directly at us, and Carolyn gripped my arm and didn't let go until he and his companion had continued on across the street.

"Jesus," she said.

"Not to worry."

"I could just picture a lightbulb forming over his head. Like in the comic strips. Are you sure he didn't recognize you?"

"Positive. Otherwise he'd have come over to the car for a closer look."

"And what would you have done?"

"I don't know. Run the light, probably."

"Jesus."

I felt the subject deserved changing. "I thought of bringing you a present," I said. "A fur jacket, really smart-looking."

"I don't like fur."

"This was a good one. It had an Arvin Tannenbaum label in it."

"Is that good?"

"He's as good as furriers get. I don't know much about furs but I know labels. This was pretty. I think it was Canada lynx. What's the matter?"

"That's a kind of a cat, Bernie. Don't tell me how pretty it was. A lynx is like a bobcat. Wearing a lynx coat would be like having lampshades made of human skin. Whether or not they're attractive is beside the point."

Another siren oogah-oogahed in the distance. An ambulance, from the sound of it. They've got ambulances these days that sound like Gestapo cars in war movies.

That last thought blended with Carolyn's lampshade image and made me ready for another change of subject. "The wig was there," I said hurriedly. "The orange one that she wore to the bookstore. So it wasn't just that my brain was addled from the drug. That was her buying Virgil's *Eclogues.*"

"She must have been afraid someone would recognize her."

I nodded. "She could have worn the wig so I wouldn't recognize her at a later meeting, but that doesn't really make much sense. I suppose she was afraid Whelkin would spot her. They must have known each other because he sent me over to her apartment, but I wish I had something more concrete to tie them together."

"Like what?"

"Pictures, for instance. I was hoping for a batch of telltale snapshots. People with a closetful of whips and chains tend to be keen Polaroid photographers. I didn't turn up a one."

"If there were any pictures, the killer could have taken them."

"Possible."

"Or maybe there weren't any to begin with. If she was only with one person at a time there wouldn't be anybody to take the pictures. Did you find a camera?"

"Nary a camera."

"Then there probably weren't any pictures."

"Probably not."

I turned into Fourteenth Street, headed west. Carolyn was looking at me oddly. I braked for a red light and turned to see her studying me, a thoughtful expression on her face.

"You know something I don't," she said.

"I know how to pick locks. That's all."

"Something else."

"It's just your imagination."

"I don't think so. You were uptight before and now you're all loose and breezy."

"It's just self-confidence and a feeling of well-being," I told her. "Don't worry. It'll pass."

❧❦❧

There was a legal parking space around the corner from her apartment, legal until 7 A.M., at any rate. I stuck the Pontiac into it and grabbed up the suitcase.

The cats met us at the door. "Good boys," Carolyn said, reaching down to pat heads. "Anybody call? Did you take messages like I taught you? Bernie, if it's not time for a drink, then the liquor ads have been misleading us for years. You game?"

"Sure."

"Scotch? Rocks? Soda?"

"Yes, yes, and no."

I unpacked my suitcase while she made the drinks, then made myself sit down and relax long enough to swallow a couple of ounces of Scotch. I waited for it to loosen some of my coiled springs, but before that could happen I was on my feet again.

Carolyn raised her eyebrows at me.

"The car," I said.

"What about it?"

"I want to put it back where I found it."

"You're kidding."

"That car's been very useful to me, Carolyn. I want to return the favor."

I paused at the door, reached back under my jacket. There was a book wedged beneath the waistband of my slacks. I drew it free and set it on a table. Carolyn looked at it and at me again.

"Something to read while I'm gone," I said.

"What is it?"

"Well," I said, "it's not Virgil's *Eclogues*."

THIRTEEN

I FELT GOOD about taking the car back. You don't spit on your luck, I told myself. I thought of stories of ballplayers refusing to change their socks while the team was on a winning streak. It was high time, I mused, to change my own socks, winning streak or no. A shower would be in order, and a change of garb.

I headed uptown on Tenth Avenue, left hand on the wheel, right hand on the seat beside me, fingers drumming idly. Somewhere in the Forties I snuck a peek at the gas gauge. I had a little less than half a tank left and I felt a need to do something nice for the car's owner, so I cut over to Eleventh Avenue and found an open station at the corner of Fifty-first Street. I had them fill the tank and check the oil while they were at it. The oil was down a quart and I had them take care of that, too.

My parking space was waiting for me on Seventy-fourth Street, but Max and his owner were nowhere to be seen. I uncoupled my jumper wire, locked up the car, and trotted back to West End Avenue to catch a southbound cab. It was still drizzling lightly but I didn't have to wait long before a cab pulled up. And it was a Checker, with room for me to stretch my legs and relax.

Things were starting to go right. I could feel it.

Out of habit, I left the cab a few blocks from Arbor Court and walked the rest of the way. I rang, and Carolyn buzzed me through the front door and met me at the door to her apartment. She put her hands on her hips and looked up at me. "You're full of surprises," she said.

"It's part of my charm."

"Uh-huh. To tell you the truth, poetry never did too much for me. I had a lover early on who thought she was Edna St. Vincent Millay and that sort of cooled me on the whole subject. Where'd you find the book?"

"The Porlock apartment."

"No shit, Bern. Here I thought you checked it out of the Jefferson Market library. Where in the apartment? Out in plain sight?"

"Uh-uh. In a shoe box on a shelf in the closet."

"It must have come as a surprise."

"I'll say. I was expecting a pair of Capezios, and look what I found."

"*The Deliverance of Fort Bucklow.* I didn't really read much of it. I skimmed the first three or four pages and I didn't figure it was going to get better."

"You were right."

"How'd you know it would be there, Bern?"

I went over to the kitchen area and made us a couple of drinks. I gave one to Carolyn and accompanied it with the admission that I hadn't known the book would be there, that I hadn't even had any particular hope of finding it. "When you don't know what you're looking for," I said, "you have a great advantage, because you don't know what you'll find."

"Just so you know it when you see it. I'm beginning to believe you lead a charmed life. First you run an ad claiming you've got the book, and then you open a shoe box and there's the book. Why did the killer stash it there?"

"He didn't. He'd have taken it with him."

"Porlock stashed it?"

"Must have. She drugged me, frisked me, grabbed the book, tucked it away in the closet, and got it hidden just in time to let her killer in the front door. She must have been alone in the apartment with me or he'd have seen her hide the book. She let him in and he killed her and left the gun in my hand and went out."

"Without the book."

"Right."

"Why would he kill her without getting the book?"

"Maybe he didn't have anything to do with the book. Maybe he had some other reason to want her dead."

"And he just happened to walk in at that particular time, and he decided to frame you because you happened to be there."

"I haven't got it all worked out yet, Carolyn."

"I can see that."

"Maybe he killed her first and started looking for the book and came up empty. Except the apartment didn't look as though it had been searched. It looked as neat as ever, except for the body on the love seat. When I came to, I mean. There was no body there tonight."

"How about the trunk of the Pontiac?"

I gave her a look. "They did leave chalkmarks, though. On the love seat and the floor, to outline where the body was. It was sort of spooky." I picked up the book and took it and my drink to the chair. Archie was curled up in it. I put down the book and the drink and moved him and sat down, and he hopped onto my lap and looked on with interest as I picked up the book again and leafed through it.

"I swear he can read," Carolyn said. "Ubi's not much on books but Archie loves to read over my shoulder. Or *under* my shoulder, come to think of it."

"A cat ought to like Kipling," I said. "Remember the *Just So Stories*? 'I am the cat who walks by himself and all places are alike to me.'"

Archie purred like a bandsaw.

"When I met you," I said, "I figured you'd have dogs."

"I'd rather go to them than have them. What made you think I was a dog person?"

"Well, the shop."

"The Poodle Factory?"

"Yeah."

"Well, what choice did I have, Bernie? I couldn't open a cat-grooming salon, for Christ's sake. Cats groom themselves."

"That's a point."

I read a little more of the book. Something bothered me. I flipped back to the flyleaf and read the hand-written inscription to H. Rider Haggard. I pictured Kipling at his desk in Surrey, dipping his pen, leaning over the book, inscribing it to his closest friend. I closed the book, turned it over and over in my hands.

"Something wrong?"

I shook my head, set the book aside, dispossessed Archie, stood up. "I'm like the cats," I announced, "and it's time I set about grooming myself. I'm going to take a shower."

❧❧❧

A while later I was sitting in the chair again. I was wearing clean clothes and I'd had a nice close shave with my own razor.

"I could get a paper," Carolyn offered. "It's after eleven. The *Times* must be out by now. The first edition."

We'd just heard the news and there wasn't anything about the Porlock murder. I pointed out that there wouldn't very likely be anything in the paper, either.

"Our ad'll be in, Bern. In the Personals."

"Where's the nearest newsstand open at this hour?"

"There's one on Greenwich Avenue but they don't get the early *Times* because they close around one or two. There's an all-night stand at the subway entrance at Fourteenth and Eighth."

"That's too far."

"I don't mind a walk."

"It's still raining and it's too far anyway, and why do we have to look at the ad?"

"To make sure it's there, I suppose."

"No point. Either somebody'll see it or they won't, and either the phone'll ring or it won't, and all we can do is wait and see what happens."

"I suppose so." She sounded wistful. "It just seems as though there ought to be something active we can do."

"The night's been active enough for me already."

"I guess you're right."

"I feel like a little blissful inactivity, to tell you the truth. I feel like sitting here feeling clean. I feel like having maybe one more drink in a few minutes and then getting ready for bed. I don't even know if people really read Personal ads in the *Times*, but I'm fairly sure they don't race for the bulldog edition so they can read about missing heirs and volunteers wanted for medical experiments."

"True."

"I'm afraid so. The phone's not going to ring for a while, Carolyn."

So of course it picked that minute to ring.

We looked at each other. Nobody moved and it went on ringing. "You get it," she said.

"Why me?"

"Because it's about the ad."

"It's not about the ad."

"Of course it's about the ad. What else would it be?"

"Maybe it's a wrong number."

"Bernie, for God's sake . . ."

I got up and answered the phone. I didn't say anything for a second, and then I said, "Hello."

No answer.

I said hello a few more times, giving the word the same flat reading each time, and I'd have gotten more of a response from Archie. I stared at the receiver for a moment, said "Hello" one final time, then said "Goodbye" and hung up.

"Interesting conversation," Carolyn said.

"It's good I answered it. It really made a difference."

"Someone wanted to find out who placed the ad. Now they've heard your voice and they know it's you."

"You're reading a lot into a moment of silence."

"Maybe I should have picked it up after all."

"And maybe what we just had was a wrong number. Or a telephone pervert. I didn't hear any heavy breathing, but maybe he's new at it."

She started to say something, then got to her feet, popping up like a toaster. "I'm gonna have one more drink," she said. "How about you?"

"A short one."

"They know it's you, Bernie. Now if they can get the address from the number—"

"They can't."

"Suppose they're the police. The police could get the phone company to cooperate, couldn't they?"

"Maybe. But what do the police know about the Kipling book?"

"I don't know."

"Well, neither do they." She handed me a drink. It was a little heftier than I'd had in mind but I didn't raise any objections. Her nervousness was contagious and I'd managed to pick up a light dose of it. I prescribed Scotch, to be followed by bed rest.

"It was probably what I said it would be when I answered it," I suggested. "A wrong number."

"You're right."

"For all we know, the ad didn't even make the early edition."

"I could take a quick run over to Fourteenth Street and check—"

"Don't be ridiculous." I picked up the book again and found myself flipping through its pages, remembering how I'd done so on an earlier occasion, sitting in my own apartment with a similar drink at hand and flushed with the triumph of a successful burglary. Well, I'd stolen the thing again, but somehow I didn't feel the same heady rush.

Something nagged at me. Some little thought out there on the edge of consciousness . . .

I finished my drink and tuned it out.

✌︎❧✌︎

Half an hour after the phone call we were bedded down for the night. *I* was bedded down, anyway; Carolyn was couched. The clock radio was supplying an undercurrent of mood music, all set to turn itself off thirty minutes into the Mantovani.

I was teetering on the edge of sleep when I half heard footsteps approaching the door of the apartment. I didn't really register them; Carolyn's was a first-floor apartment, after all, and various feet had been approaching it all night long, only to pass it and continue on up the stairs. This time the steps stopped outside the door, and just as that fact was beginning to penetrate I heard a key in the lock.

I sat up in bed. The key turned in the lock. Beside me, a cat sat quivering with excitement. As another key slipped into another of the locks, Carolyn stirred on the couch and whispered my name urgently.

We were both on our feet by the time the door opened. A hand reached in to switch on the overhead light. We stood there blinking.

"I'm dreaming," Randy said. "None of this is really happening."

Shoulder-length chestnut hair. A high broad forehead, a long oval face. Large eyes, larger now than I'd ever seen them, and a mouth in the shape of the letter O.

"Jesus," Carolyn said. "Randy, it's not what you think."

"Of course not. The two of you were playing canasta. You had the lights out so you wouldn't disturb the cats. Why else would you be wearing your Dr. Denton's, Carolyn? And does Bernie like the handy drop seat?"

"You've got it all wrong."

"I know. It's terrible the way I jump to conclusions. At least you're dressed warmly. Bernie, poor thing, you're shivering in your undershorts. Why don't the two of you huddle together for warmth, Carolyn? It wouldn't bother me a bit."

"Randy, you just don't understand."

"You're dead right about that. I figured you knew what you were by now. Aren't you a little old for a sexual-identity crisis?"

"Dammit, Randy—"

"Dammit is right. Dammit is definitely right. I *thought* I recognized Bernie's voice on the telephone. And I was struck tongue-tied. After I hung up I told myself it was probably innocent, the two of you are friends, and I asked myself why I reacted with such paranoia. But you know what they say, Carolyn. Just because you're paranoid doesn't mean real little people aren't following you."

"Will you please listen to me?"

"No, *you* listen to *me*, you little shit. What I said was, well, screw it, Miranda, you've got a key, so go over and join the two of them and see how silly you're being, or maybe you'll get lucky and Carolyn'll be alone and you can have some laughs and patch things up, and— God *damn* you, Carolyn. Here's your set of keys, bitch. I won't walk in on you two again. Count on it."

"Randy, I—"

"I said here's your keys. And I think you have *my* keys, Carolyn, and I'd like them back. Now, if you don't mind."

We tried to say something but it was pointless. There was nothing she wanted to hear. She gave back Carolyn's keys and pocketed her own and stormed out, slamming the door hard enough to rattle the dishes on the kitchen table, stamping her way down the hall, slamming the vestibule door on her way out of the building.

Carolyn and I just stood there looking at each other.

Ubi had gone to hide under the bed. Archie stood up on the chair and let out a tentative yowl. After a couple of minutes Carolyn went over to the door and set about locking the locks.

FOURTEEN

THE PERSONAL ADS were on the penultimate page of the second section of the *Times*, along with the shipping news and a few other high-priority items. Ours was the third listing, following a plea for information from the parents of a fourteen-year-old runaway.

I read our ad three or four times and decided that it did its job efficiently enough. It hadn't brought any response yet, but it was still early; Carolyn had awakened at dawn and gone for the paper as soon as she'd fed the cats. At this hour our presumably interested parties might well be snug in their beds. If, like me and Carolyn, they were already warming themselves over morning coffee, they'd still have the whole paper to wade through before they got to the Personals. True, it was a Saturday. The daily *Times* has added on feature sections in recent years, padding itself like a bear preparing to hibernate, but the Saturday paper remains fashionably slender. On the other hand, a good many people take a break from the *Times* on Saturdays, readying themselves for the onslaught of the enormous Sunday paper, so it was possible our prospective customers would never pick up the paper at all. The ad was set to run for a week, but now that I looked at it, a few lines of type on a remote back page, I wasn't too cocky about the whole thing. We couldn't really count on it, I decided, and it would be advisable to draft a backup plan as soon as possible.

"Oh, wow. I'm glad I went out for the paper, Bernie."

"So am I," I said. "I just hope you're not the only person who took the trouble."

She had the first section and she was pointing to something. "You'd better read this," she said.

I took it and read it. A few inches of copy on one of the back pages, out of place among the scraps of international news but for its faintly international flavor. Bernard Rhodenbarr, I read, the convicted burglar currently sought by police investigating the slaying Thursday of Madeleine Porlock in her East Side apartment, had narrowly escaped apprehension the previous night. Surprised by an alert police officer while attempting to break into Barnegat Books on East Eleventh Street, Rhodenbarr whipped out a pistol and exchanged shots with the policeman. The officer, I read, suffered a flesh wound to the foot and was treated at St. Vincent's Hospital and released. The burglar-turned-gunman, owner of the store in question, had escaped on foot, apparently uninjured.

As an afterthought, the last paragraph mentioned that Rhodenbarr had disguised himself for the occasion by donning a turban and false beard. "But he didn't fool me," Patrolman Francis Rockland was quoted as saying. "We're trained to see past obvious disguises. I recognized him right away from his photograph."

"The Sikh," I told Carolyn. "Well, that's one person who hasn't got the book, or he wouldn't have been trying to break into the store to search for it. I wonder if it was him you spotted watching the store yesterday."

"Maybe."

"The tabloids'll probably give this more of a play. They like irony, and what's more ironic than a burglar caught breaking into his own place? They should only know how ironic it is."

"What do you mean?"

"Well, the cop could have arrested the Sikh. That wouldn't have cleared me on the murder rap but at least they wouldn't be after me for this, too. Or the Sikh could have been a worse shot, so I wouldn't be charged with shooting a cop. Wounding a police officer is a more serious crime than murdering a civilian, at least as far as the cops are concerned. Or, if he had to shoot him, the Sikh could have *killed* young Mr. Rockland. Then he wouldn't have been able to tell them I was the one who did it."

"You wouldn't really want the policeman dead, Bernie."

"No. With my luck he'd live long enough to tell a brother officer who shot him. Then I'd be a cop killer. What if Randy sees this? She must have missed the first story, or at least she never connected it with me, because she didn't seem concerned last night about your harboring a fugitive. She was too busy feeling betrayed."

"She never looks at the *Times*."

"It'll be in the other papers, too."

"She probably won't read them, either. I don't even know if she knows your last name."

"She must."

"Maybe."

"Would she call the cops?"

"She's a good person, Bernie. She's not a fink."

"She's also jealous. She thinks—"

"I know what she thinks. She must be a lunatic to think it, but I know what she thinks."

"She could decide to give the cops an anonymous tip. She could tell herself it was for your own good, Carolyn."

"Shit." She gnawed a thumbnail. "You figure it's not safe here anymore?"

"I don't know."

"But the phone's here. And the number's in the paper, and how are we going to answer it from a distance?"

"Who's going to call, anyway?"

"Rudyard Whelkin."

"He killed Madeleine Porlock Thursday night. I'll bet he took a cab straight to Kennedy and was out of the country by midnight."

"Without the book?"

I shrugged.

"And the Sikh might call. What happened to his five hundred dollars?"

"You figure he'll call so he can ask me that question?"

"No, I'm asking it, Bern. You had the money on you when Madeleine Porlock drugged you, right?"

"Right."

"And it was gone when you came to."

"Right again."

"So what happened to it?"

"She took it. *Oh.* What happened to it *after* she took it?"

"Yeah. Where did it go? You went through her things last night. It wasn't stashed with the book, was it?"

"It wasn't stashed anywhere. Nowhere that I looked, that is. I suppose the killer took it along with him."

"Wouldn't he leave it?"

"Why leave money? Money's money, Carolyn."

"There's always stories about killings in the paper, and they say the police ruled out robbery as a motive because the victim had a large sum of cash on his person."

"That's organized crime. They want people to know why they killed somebody. They'll even plant money on a person so the police will rule out robbery. Either the killer took the money this time or Porlock found a hiding place that didn't occur to me. Or some cop picked it up when no one was looking. That's been known to happen."

"Really?"

"Oh, sure. I could tell you no end of stories. But what's the point? I'd be interrupted by the insistent ringing of the telephone."

And I turned to the instrument, figuring it would recognize a cue when it heard one. It stayed silent, though, for upwards of half an hour.

But once it started ringing, I didn't think it was ever going to stop.

Rrrring!

"Hello?"

"Ah, hello. I've just read your notice in the *Times*. I'm only wondering if I'm interpreting it correctly."

"How are you interpreting it?"

"You would appear to have something to sell."

"That's correct."

"Passage to, ah, Fort Bucklow."

"Yes."

"Would it be possible for me to know to whom I am speaking?"

"I was going to ask you that very question."

"Ah. An impasse. Let me consider this."

An English inflection, an undertone of Asia or Africa.

A slightly sibilant *s*. Educated, soft-spoken. A pleasant voice, all in all.

"Very well, sir. I believe you may already have encountered an emissary of mine. If my guess is right, you overcharged him in a transaction recently. He paid five hundred dollars for a book priced at a dollar ninety-five."

"Not my fault. He ran off without his change."

An appreciative chuckle. "Then you are the man I assumed you to be. Very good. You have pluck, sir. The police seek you in connection with a woman's death and you persist in your efforts to sell a book. Business as usual, eh?"

"I need money right now."

"To quit the country, I would suppose. You have the book at hand? It is actually in your possession as we talk?"

"Yes. I don't believe I caught your name."

"I don't believe I've given it. Before we go further, sir, perhaps you could prove to me that you have the volume."

"I suppose I could hold it to the phone, but unless you have extraordinary powers . . ."

"Open it to page forty-two, sir, and read the first stanza on the page."

"Oh. Hold on a minute. 'Now if you should go to Fort Bucklow / When the moon is on the wane, / And the jackal growls while the monkey howls / Like a woman struck insane . . .' Is that the one you mean?"

A pause. "I want that volume, sir. I want to buy it."

"Good. I want to sell it."

"And your price?"

"I haven't set it yet."

"If you will do so . . ."

"This is tricky business. I have to protect myself. I'm

a fugitive, as you said, and that makes me vulnerable. I don't even know whom I'm dealing with."

"A visitor in your land, sir. A passionate devotee of Mr. Kipling. My name is of little importance."

"How can I get in touch with you?"

"It's of less importance than my name. I can get in touch with *you*, sir, by calling this number."

"No. I won't be here. It's not safe. Give me a number where I can reach you at five o'clock this afternoon."

"A telephone number?"

"Yes."

"I can't do that."

"It can be any telephone at all. Just so you'll be at it at five o'clock."

"Ah. I will call you back, sir, in ten minutes."

Rrrring!

"Hello?"

"Sir, you have pencil and paper?"

"Go ahead."

"I will be at this number at five o'clock this afternoon. RH4-5198."

"RH4-5198. At five o'clock."

Rrrring! Rrrring!

"Hello?"

"Hello?"

"Hello."

"Ah. If you could say something more elaborate than a simple *hello* . . ."

"What do you want me to say?"

"Very good. I'd hoped it was you. I won't use your name aloud, and I trust you won't use mine."

"Only if I want to call your club and have you paged."

"Don't do that."

"They said you weren't a member. Extraordinary, isn't it?"

"Perhaps I haven't been altogether straightforward with you, my boy. I can explain everything."

"I'm sure you can."

"The elusive item. Can I assume from your advertisement that it hasn't slipped out of your hands?"

"It's in front of me even as we speak."

"Excellent."

" 'Now if you should go to Fort Bucklow / When the moon is on the wane, / And the jackal growls while the monkey howls . . .' "

"For heaven's sake, don't *read* it to me. Or have you committed great stretches of it to memory?"

"No, I was reading."

"Oh, to prove possession? Hardly necessary, my boy. You'd scarcely have shot the woman and then left the book behind, would you? Now how are we going to manage this transaction?"

"We could meet someplace."

"We could. Of course neither of us would welcome the attention of the police. I wonder . . ."

"Give me a number where I can reach you at six o'clock."

"Why don't I simply call you?"

"Because I don't know where I'll be."

"I see. Well, my boy, at the risk of appearing to play

them close to the vest, I'm not sure I'd care to give out
this number."

"Any number, then."

"How's that?"

"Pick a pay phone. Give me the number and be there
to answer it at six."

"Ah. I'll get back to you."

Rrrring!

"Hello?"

"CHelsea 2-9419."

"Good."

"At six o'clock."

"Good."

Rrrring!

"Hello?"

"Hello. I believe you advertised—"

"Passage to Fort Bucklow. That's correct."

"May I speak frankly? We're talking about a book, are
we not?"

"Yes."

"And you wish to purchase it?"

"I have it for sale."

A pause. "I see. You actually own a copy. You have it
in your possession."

" '. . . The jackal growls while the monkey howls /
Like a woman struck insane . . .' "

"What did you say?"

"I'm reading from the top of page forty-two."

"That would hardly seem necessary." Another pause. "This is confusing. Perhaps I should give you my name."

"That'd be nice."

"It's Demarest. Prescott Demarest, and I don't suppose it will mean anything to you. I'm acting as agent for a wealthy collector whose name would mean something to you, but I haven't the authority to mention it. He was recently offered a copy of this book. The offer was suddenly withdrawn. I wonder if it's the same copy?"

"I couldn't say."

"The copy he was offered was represented as unique. It was our understanding that only one copy of the book exists."

"Then it must be the same copy."

"So it would seem. I don't think you gave your name."

"I'm careful about my privacy, Mr. Demarest. Like your employer."

"I see. I'd have to consult him, of course, but if you could let me know your price?"

"It hasn't been set yet."

"There are other potential buyers?"

"Several."

"I'd like to see the book. Before you offer it to anyone else. If we could arrange to meet—"

"I can't talk right now, Mr. Demarest. Where can I reach you this afternoon at, say, four o'clock? Will you be near a telephone?"

"I can arrange to be."

"Could I have the number?"

"I don't see why not. Take this down. WOrth 4-1114. You did say four o'clock? I'll expect to hear from you then."

"I think that's it," I told Carolyn, after I'd summa-
rized the Demarest conversation for her. "I don't think
there are going to be any more calls."

"How can you tell?"

"I can't, but it's one of my stronger hunches. The first
caller was foreign and he's the one who sicced the Sikh
on me. The Sikh came around Thursday afternoon, so
he's known at least that long that I had the book, but he
made me read it to him over the phone."

"What does that prove?"

"Beats me. Right now I'm just piling up data. Interpreting it will have to wait. The second call was from
Whelkin and he wasn't terribly interested in howling
jackals or growling monkeys."

"I think it's the other way around."

"Monkeys and jackals aren't terribly interested in
Whelkin?"

"The jackal was growling and the monkey was howling. Not that it makes a hell of a lot of difference. What
are you getting at, Bernie?"

"Good question. Whelkin seemed to take it for
granted that I killed Madeleine Porlock. That's why he
wasn't surprised I had the book. Which means he didn't
kill her. Unless, of course, he was pretending to believe I
killed her, in which case . . ."

"In which case what?"

"Damned if I know. That leaves Demarest, and
there's something refreshing about him. He was very
open about his name and he didn't have to be coaxed
into supplying his phone number. What do you suppose
that means?"

"I don't know."

"Neither do I." I helped myself to more coffee. "The murder's what screws things up. If somebody hadn't killed Madeleine Porlock I wouldn't have a problem. Or if the police weren't looking to hang the killing on me. I'd just sell the book to the highest bidder and spend the next two weeks in the Bahamas. One of those three killed her, Carolyn."

"One of the ones who just called?"

"Uh-huh." I looked at my watch. "We don't have a hell of a lot of time," I said. "I'm supposed to call them at hourly intervals, starting with Demarest at four. That gives us a couple of hours to set things up."

"To set what up?"

"A trap. It's going to be tricky, though, because I don't know who to set it for or what to use for bait. There's only one thing to do."

"What's that?"

"What I always do in time of stress," I said. "Bribe a cop."

FIFTEEN

WHEN HE CAME to the phone I apologized for the intrusion. "Your wife didn't want to disturb you," I said, "but I told her it was important."

"Well, I got Wake Forest and ten points," he said. "So all I been doin' is watch twenty bucks go down the chute."

"Who are they playing?"

"University of Georgia. The Bulldogs got what they call the Junkyard Dog defense. All it means is they're chewin' the ass offa poor Wake Forest." There was a long and thoughtful pause. "Who the hell," he said, "*is* this?"

"Just an old friend and enemy who needs a favor."

"Jesus, it's you. Kid, I seen you step in it before, but I swear this time you got both feet smack in the middle of God's birthday cake. Where are you callin' from, anyway?"

"The Slough of Despond. I need a favor, Ray."

"Jesus, that's the truth. Well, you came to the right place. You want me to set up a surrender, right? First smart move you made since you iced the Porlock dame. You stay out there and it's just a question of time before somebody tags you, and what do you want to get shot for? And the word is shoot first on you, Bern." He clucked at me. "That wasn't too brilliant, you know. Shootin' a cop. The department takes a dim view."

"I never shot him."

"C'mon, kid. He was there, right? He saw you."

"He saw a clown with a beard and a turban. I never shot him and I never shot her either."

"And all you do is sell books. You told me the whole story, remember? How you're straight as a javelin and all? Listen, you'll be okay now. I'll set up a surrender, and don't think I don't appreciate it. Makes me look good, no question about it, and it saves your ass. You get yourself a decent lawyer and who knows, you might even beat the whole thing in court. Worst comes to worst, so you do a couple of years upstate. You done that before."

"Ray, I never—"

"One thing that's not so good, this Rockland kid's young and feisty, you know? If it was an old-timer you shot, he'd probably take a couple of kay to roll over in court and fudge the testimony. 'Course, if it was an old-timer, he probably woulda shot you instead of waitin' to get hisself shot in the foot. So I guess you break even on that one, Bern."

We went a few more rounds, me proclaiming my innocence while he told me how I could cop a plea and probably get off with writing "I won't steal no more" one hundred times on the blackboard after school. Eventually I shifted gears and told him there was something specific I wanted from him.

"Oh?"

"I have three phone numbers. I want you to run them down for me."

"You nuts, Bernie? You know what's involved in tracin' a call? You gotta set up in advance, you gotta be able to reach somebody at the phone company on another line, and then you gotta keep the mark on the

phone for a couple of minutes and even then they sometimes can't make the trace work. And then if you—"

"I already know the three numbers, Ray."

"Huh?"

"I know the numbers, I want to know the locations of
the phones. As if I already traced the calls successfully
and I want to know where I traced them to."

"Oh."

"You could do that, couldn't you?"

He thought it over. "Sure," he said, "but why should
I?"

I gave him a very good reason.

"I don't know," he said, after we'd discussed my very
good reason for a few minutes. "Seems to me I'm takin' a
hell of a chance."

"What chance? You'll make a phone call, that's all."

"Meanwhile I'm cooperatin' with a fugitive from jus-
tice. That's not gonna go down too good if anybody ever
hears about it."

"Who's going to hear?"

"You never know. Another thing, how in the hell are
you ever gonna deliver? You make it sound good, but
how can you deliver? If some rookie with high marks on
the pistol range whacks you out, Bern, where does that
leave me?"

"It leaves you alive. Think where it leaves me."

"That's why I'm sayin' you oughta surrender."

"Nobody's going to shoot me," I said, with perhaps a
shade more confidence than I possessed. "And I'll deliver
what I promised. When did I ever let you down?"

"Well . . ."

"Ray, all you have to do is make a phone call or two.
Isn't it worth a shot? For Christ's sake, if Wake Forest is
worth a twenty-dollar investment—"

"Don't remind me. My money's gurglin' down the drain and I'm not even watchin' it go."

"Look at the odds I'm giving you. All you got with Wake Forest is ten points."

"Yeah." I listened while his mental wheels spun. "You ever tell anybody we had this conversation—"

"You know me better than that, Ray."

"Yeah, you're all right. Okay, gimme the numbers."

I gave them to him and he repeated them in turn.

"All right," he said. "Now gimme the number where you're at and I'll get back to you soon as I can."

"Sure," I said. "The number here." I was about to read it off the little disc on the telephone when Carolyn grabbed my arm and showed me a face overflowing with alarm. "Uh, I don't think so," I told Ray. "If it's that easy for you to find out where a phone's located—"

"Bern, what kind of a guy do you think I am?"

I let that one glide by. "Besides," I said, "I'm on my way out the door, anyway. Best thing is if I call you back. How much time do you need?"

"Depends what kind of cooperation I get from the phone company."

"Say half an hour?"

"Yeah," he said. "Sounds good. Try me in half an hour, Bernie."

꒰ ꒱

I cradled the receiver. Carolyn and both cats were looking at me expectantly. "A camera," I said.

"Huh?"

"We've got half an hour to get a camera. A Polaroid, actually, unless you know somebody with a darkroom, and who wants to screw around developing film? We need a Polaroid. I don't suppose you've got one?"

"No."

"Is there one you could borrow? I hate the idea of running out and buying one. The midtown stores are likely to be crowded and I don't even know if there's a camera place in the Village. There's stores on Fourteenth Street but the stuff they sell tends to fall apart on the way home. And there's pawnshops on Third Avenue but I hate to make the rounds over there with a price on my head. Of course you could go over there and buy one."

"If I knew what to buy. I'd hate to get it home and find out it doesn't work. What do we need a camera for, anyway?"

"To take some pictures."

"I never would have thought of that. It's a shame Randy walked in when she did. She's got one of those new Polaroids, you take the picture and it's developed before you can let go of the shutter."

"Randy's got a Polaroid?"

"That's what I just said. Didn't I show you pictures of the cats last week?"

"Probably."

"Well, she took them. But I can't ask her to borrow it, because she's convinced we're having an affair and she'd probably think I wanted us to take obscene pictures of each other or something. And she's probably not home, anyway."

"Call her and see."

"Are you kidding? I don't want to talk to her."

"Hang up if she answers."

"Then why call in the first place?"

"Because if she's *not* home," I said, "we can go pick up the camera."

"Beautiful." She reached for the phone, then sighed and let her hand drop. "You're forgetting something. Remember last night? I gave her keys back."

"So?"

"Huh?"

"Who needs keys?"

She looked at me, laughed, shook her head. "Far out," she said, and reached for the phone.

ひえ

Randy lived in a tiny studio on the fifth floor of a squat brick apartment house on Morton Street between Seventh Avenue and Hudson. There's an article in the New York building code requiring an elevator in every structure of seven or more stories. This one was six stories tall, and up the stairs we went.

The locks were candy. They wouldn't have been much trouble if I'd been limited to my drugstore tools. Now that I had my pro gear, I went through them like the Wehrmacht through Luxembourg. When the penny dropped and the final lock snicked open, I looked up at Carolyn. Her mouth was wide open and her blue eyes were larger than I'd ever seen them.

"God," she said. "It takes me longer than that when I've got the keys."

"Well, they're cheap locks. And I was showing off a little. Trying to impress you."

"It worked. I'm impressed."

We were in and out quicker than Speedy Gonzales. The camera was where Carolyn thought it would be, in the bottom drawer of Randy's dresser. It nestled in a carrying case with a shoulder strap, and an ample supply of film reposed in the case's zippered film compartment.

Carolyn slung the thing over her shoulder, I locked the locks, and we were on our way home.

⌣⌢⌣

I'd told Ray I would call him in half an hour and I didn't miss by more than a few minutes. He answered the phone himself this time. "Your friend moves around," he said.

"Huh?"

"The guy with the three phone numbers. He covers a lot of ground. The Rhinelander number's a sidewalk pay phone on the corner of Seventy-fifth and Madison. The Chelsea number's also a pay phone. It's located in the lobby of the Gresham Hotel. That's on Twenty-third between Fifth and Sixth."

"Hold on," I said, scribbling furiously. "All right. How about the Worth number?"

"Downtown. I mean way downtown, in the Wall Street area. Twelve Pine Street."

"Another lobby phone?"

"Nope. An office on the fourteenth floor. A firm called Tontine Trading Corp. Bern, let's get back to the coat, huh? You said ranch mink, didn't you?"

"That's right."

"What did you say the color was?"

"Silver-blue."

"And it's full-fashioned? You're sure of that?"

"Positive. You can't go wrong with this one, Ray. It's carrying an Arvin Tannenbaum label, and that's strictly carriage trade."

"When can I have it?"

"In plenty of time for Christmas, Ray. No problem."

"You son of a bitch. What are you givin' me? You haven't got the coat."

"Of course not. I retired, Ray. I gave up burglary. What would I be doing with a hot coat?"

"Then where'd the coat come from?"

"I'm going to get it for you, Ray. After I get myself out of the jam I'm in."

"Suppose you don't get out of it, Bern? Then what?"

"Well, you better hope I do," I said, "or else the coat's down the same chute as your twenty-buck bet on Wake Forest."

SIXTEEN

I CABBED UPTOWN for the Pontiac. By the time I brought it downtown again Carolyn had familiarized herself with the intricacies of the Polaroid camera. She proved this by clicking the shutter at me as I came through the door. The picture popped out and commenced developing before my eyes. I looked startled, and guilty of something or other. I told Carolyn I wasn't going to order any enlargements.

"You're a better model than the cats," she said. "Ubi wouldn't sit still and Archie kept crossing his eyes."

"Archie always keeps crossing his eyes."

"It's part of being Burmese. Wanna take my picture?"

"Sure."

She was wearing a charcoal-gray turtleneck and slate-blue corduroy jeans. For the photo she slipped on a brass-buttoned blazer and topped things off with a rakish beret. So attired, she sat on the edge of a table, crossed her legs, and grinned at the camera like an endearing waif.

Randy's Polaroid captured all of this remarkably well. We studied the result together. "What's missing," Carolyn said, "is a cigar."

"You don't smoke cigars."

"To pose with. It'd make me look very *Bonnie and Clyde.*"

"Which of them do you figure you'd look like?"

"Oh, very funny. Nothing like a little sexist humor to lighten the mood. Are we ready to go?"

"I think so. You've got the Blinns' bracelet?"

"In my pocket."

"And you're comfortable with the camera?"

"It's about as tricky to operate as a self-service elevator."

"Then let's go."

And on the sidewalk I said, "Uh, Carolyn, you may not remind anybody of Faye Dunaway, but you look terrific today."

"What's all this about?"

"And you're not bad to have around, either."

"What *is* this? A speech to the troops before going into battle?"

"Something like that, I guess."

"Well, watch it, will you? I could get misty-eyed and run my mascara. It's a good thing I don't wear any. Can't you drive this crate, Bern?"

❧❦❧

On weekends, New York's financial district looks as though someone zapped it with one of those considerate bombs that kills people without damaging property. Narrow streets, tall buildings, and no discernible human activity whatsoever. All the shops were closed, all the people home watching football games.

I left the Pontiac in an unattended parking lot on Nassau and we walked down to Pine. Number 12 was an office building that towered above those on either side of it. A guard sat at a desk in the lobby, logging the handful of workers who refused to let the weekend qualify their devotion to the pursuit of profit.

We stood on the far side of Pine for eight or ten minutes, during which time the attendant had nothing whatever to do. No one signed in or out. I looked up and counted nine lighted windows on the front of the building. I tried to determine if one of these might be on the fourteenth floor, a process made somewhat more difficult by the angle at which I had to gaze and the impossibility of determining which was the fourteenth floor, since I had no way of knowing if the building had a thirteenth floor.

I couldn't find a pay phone in line of sight of the building. I went around the corner and walked a block up William Street. At two minutes past four I dialed the number Prescott Demarest had given me. He picked it up after it had rung twice but didn't say anything until I'd said hello myself. If I'd shown similar restraint the night before we could have had Randy's Polaroid without breaking and entering to get it.

"I have the book," I told him. "And I need cash. I have to leave town. If you're ready to deal, I can offer you a bargain."

"I'll pay a fair price. If I'm convinced the item is genuine."

"Suppose I show it to you tonight? If you decide you want it, then we can work out a price."

"Tonight?"

"At Barnegat Books. That's a store on East Eleventh Street."

"I know where it is. There was a story in this morning's paper—"

"I know."

"You feel it's entirely safe? Meeting at this store?"

"I think so. There's no police surveillance, if that's worrying you. I checked earlier this afternoon." And so I had, driving past slowly in the Pontiac. "Eleven o'clock," I said. "I'll see you then."

I hung up and walked back to the corner of William and Pine. I could see the entrance of Number 12 from there, though not terribly well. I'd left Carolyn directly across the street in the doorway of a shop that offered old prints and custom framing. I couldn't tell if she was still there or not.

I stayed put for maybe five minutes. Then someone emerged from the building, walking off immediately toward Nassau Street. He'd no sooner disappeared from view than Carolyn stepped out from the printshop's doorway and gave me a wave.

I sprinted back to the telephone, dialed WOrth 4-1114. I let it ring a full dozen times, hung up, retrieved my dime, and raced back to where Carolyn was waiting. "No answer," I told her. "He's left the office."

"Then we've got his picture."

"There was just the one man?"

"Uh-huh. Somebody else left earlier, but you hadn't even gotten to the phone by then, so I didn't bother taking his picture. Then one man came out, and I waved to you after I snapped him, and there hasn't been anybody since then. Here's somebody now. It's a woman. Should I take her picture?"

"Don't bother."

"She's signing out. Demarest didn't bother. He just waved to the guard and walked on by."

"Doesn't mean anything. I've done that myself, hitting doormen with the old nonchalance. If you act like they know you, they figure they must."

"Here's his picture. What we really need is one of those zoom lenses or whatever you call them. At least this is a narrow street or you wouldn't be able to see much."

I studied the picture. It didn't have the clarity of a Bachrach portrait but the lighting was good and Demarest's face showed up clearly. He was a big man, middle-aged, with the close-cropped gray hair of a retired Marine colonel.

The face was vaguely familiar but I couldn't think why. He was no one I'd ever seen before.

On the way uptown Carolyn used the rear-view mirror to check the angle of her beret. It took a few minutes before she was satisfied with it.

"That was really funny," she said.

"Taking Demarest's picture?"

"What's funny about taking somebody's picture? It wasn't even scary. I had visions of him coming straight across the street and braining me with the camera, but he never even noticed. Just a quiet little click from the shadows. No, I was talking about last night."

"Oh."

"When Randy turned up. The ultimate bedroom farce. I swear, if jumping weren't allowed she'd never get to a conclusion."

"Well, from her point of view—"

"Oh, the whole thing's ridiculous from anybody's point of view. But there's one thing you've got to admit."

"What's that?"

"She's really cute when she's mad."

By a quarter to five we were in a cocktail lounge called Sangfroid. It was as elegant as the surrounding neighborhood, its floor deeply carpeted, its décor running to black wood and chrome. Our table was a black disc eighteen inches in diameter. Our chairs were black vinyl hemispheres with chrome bases. My drink was Perrier water with ice and lime. Carolyn's was a martini.

"I know you don't drink when you work," she said. "But this isn't drinking."

"What is it?"

"Therapy. And not a moment too soon, because I think I'm hallucinating. Do you see what I see?"

"I see a very tall gentleman with a beard and a turban walking south on Madison Avenue."

"Does that mean we're both hallucinating?"

I shook my head. "The chap's a Sikh," I said. "Unless he's a notorious homicidal burglar wearing a fiendishly clever disguise."

"What's he doing?"

He had entered the telephone booth. It was on our corner, a matter of yards from where we sat, and we could see him quite clearly through the window. I couldn't swear he was the same Sikh who'd held a gun on me, but the possibility certainly did suggest itself.

"Is he the man who called you?"

"I don't think so."

"Then why's he in the booth? He's ten minutes early, anyway."

"Maybe his watch is fast."

"Is he just going to sit there? Wait a minute. Who's he calling?"

"I don't know. If it's Dial-A-Prayer, you might get the number from him."

"It's not Dial-A-Prayer. He's saying something."

"Maybe it's Dial-A-Mantra and he's chanting along with the recording."

"He's hanging up."

"So he is," I said.

"And going away."

But not far. He crossed the street and took a position in the doorway of a boutique. He was about as inconspicuous as the World Trade Center.

"He's standing guard," I said. "I think he just checked to make sure the coast was clear. Then he called the man I spoke with earlier and told him as much. Those may have been his very words—*The coast is clear*—but somehow I doubt it. Here comes our man now, I think."

"Where did he come from?"

"The Carlyle, probably. It's just a block away, and where else would you stay if you were the sort to employ turbaned Sikhs? The Waldorf, perhaps, if you had a sense of history. The Sherry-Netherland, possibly, if you were a film producer and the Sikh was Yul Brynner in drag. The Pierre maybe, just maybe, if—"

"It's definitely him. He's in the booth."

"So he is."

"Now what?"

I stood up, found a dime in my pocket, checked my watch. "It's about that time," I said. "You'll excuse me, won't you? I have a call to make."

∽᠀᠀

It was a longish call. A couple of times the operator cut in to ask for nickels, and it wasn't the sort of conversation where one welcomed the intrusion. I thought of setting the receiver down, walking a few dozen yards, tapping on the phone-booth door and hanging onto my nickels. I decided that would be pound foolish.

I hung up, finally, and the operator rang back almost immediately to ask for a final dime. I dropped it in, then stood there fingering my ring of picks and probes and having fantasies of opening the coin box and retrieving what I'd spent. I'd never tried to pick a telephone, the game clearly not being worth the candle, but how hard could it be? I studied the key slot for perhaps a full minute before coming sharply to my senses.

Carolyn would love that one, I thought, and hurried back to the table to fill her in. She wasn't there. I sat for a moment. The ice had melted in my Perrier and the natural carbonation, while remarkably persistent, was clearly flagging. I gazed out the window. The phone booth on the corner was empty, and I couldn't spot the Sikh in the doorway across the street.

Had she responded to a call of nature? If so, she'd toted the camera along with her. I gave her an extra minute to return from the ladies' room; then laid a five-dollar bill atop the little table, weighted it down with my glass, and got out of there.

I took another look for the Sikh and still couldn't find him. I crossed the street and walked north on Madison in the direction of the Carlyle. Bobby Short was back from his summer break, I seemed to recall reading, and Tommy Flanagan, Ella Fitzgerald's accompanist for years, was doing a solo act in the Bemelmans Lounge. It struck me that I couldn't think of a nicer way to spend a New York evening, and that I hadn't been getting out much of late, and once this mess was cleared up I'd have to pay another visit to this glittering neighborhood.

Unless, of course, this mess didn't get cleared up. In

which case I wouldn't be getting out much for years on end.

I was entertaining this grim thought when a voice came at me from a doorway on my left. "Pssssst," I heard. "Hey, Mac, wanna buy a hot camera?"

And there she was, a cocky grin on her face. "You found me," she said.

"I'm keen and resourceful."

"And harder to shake than a summer cold."

"That too. I figured you were in the john. When you failed to return, I took action."

"So did I. I tried taking his picture while you were talking to him. From our table. All I got was reflections. You couldn't even tell if there was anyone inside the telephone booth."

"So you went out and waylaid him."

"Yeah. I figured when he was done he'd probably go back where he came from, so I found this spot and waited for him. Either he made more calls or you were talking a long time."

"We were talking a long time."

"Then he showed up, finally, and he never even noticed me. He passed close by, too. Look at this."

"A stunning likeness."

"That's nothing. The film popped out the way it does, and I watched it develop, and it's really amazing the way it does that, and then I tore it off and put it in my pocket, and I popped out of the doorway, ready to go back and look for you, and who do you think I bumped into?"

"Rudyard Whelkin."

"Is he around here? Did you see him?"

"No."

"Then why did you say that?"

"Just a guess. Let's see. Prescott Demarest?"

"No. What's the matter with you, Bern? It was the Sikh."

"That would have been my third guess."

"Well, you would have been right. I popped out with my camera in my hot little hands and I almost smacked right into him. He looked down at me and I looked up at him, and I'll tell you, Bernie, I could have used a step-stool."

"What happened?"

"What happened is I was incredibly brilliant. A mind like quicksilver. I went all saucer-eyed and I said, 'Oh, wow, a turban! Are you from India, sir? Are you with the United Nations? Gosh, will you pose for me so I can take your picture?' "

"How did this go over?"

"Smashingly. Look for yourself."

"You're getting pretty handy with that camera."

"You're no more impressed than he was. He's going to buy himself a Polaroid first thing Monday morning. I had to take two pictures, incidentally, because he wanted one for a souvenir. Turn it over, Bernie. Read the back."

An elegant inscription, with lots of curlicues and nonfunctional loops and whorls. *To my tiny princess / With devotion and esteem / Your loyal servant / Atman Singh.*

"That's his name," she explained. "Atman Singh."

"I figured that."

"Clever of you. The guy you were on the phone with is Atman Singh's boss, which you also probably figured. The boss's name is— Well, come to think of it, I don't know his name, but his title is the Maharajah of Ranchipur. But I suppose you knew that too, huh?"

"No," I said softly. "I didn't know that."

"They're at the Carlyle, you were right about that. The Maharajah likes to take people with him when he travels. Especially women. I had the feeling I could have joined the party if I played my cards right."

"I wonder how you'd look with a ruby in your navel."

"A little too femme, don't you think? Anyway, Atman Singh likes me just the way I am."

"So do I." I put a hand on her shoulder. "You did beautifully, Carolyn. I'm impressed."

"So am I," she said, "if I say so myself. But it wasn't just me alone. I could never have done it without the martini."

❧❦❧

Driving south and east, she said, "It was exciting, doing that number with Atman Singh. At first I was scared and then I didn't even notice I was scared because I was so completely into it. Do you know what I mean?"

"Of course I know what you mean. I get the same feeling in other people's houses."

"Yeah, that was a kick. In Randy's place. I never realized burglary could be thrilling like that. Now I can see how people might do it primarily for the kick, with the money secondary."

"When you're a pro," I said, "the money's never secondary."

"I guess not. She was really jealous, wasn't she?"

"Randy?"

"Yeah. Hey, when this is all over, maybe you could teach me a few things."

"Like what?"

"Like opening locks without keys. If you think I could learn."

"Well, there's a certain amount a person can learn. I think there's a knack for lockpick work that you either have or you don't, but beyond that there are things I could teach you."

"How about starting a car without a key?"

"Jumping the ignition? That's a cinch. You could learn that in ten minutes."

"I don't drive, though."

"That does make it a pointless skill to acquire."

"Yeah, but I'd sort of like to be able to do it. Just for the hell of it. Hey, Bern?"

"What?"

She made a fist, punched me lightly on the upper arm. "I know this is like life and death," she said, "but I'm having a good time. I just wanted to tell you that."

❧❦❧

By five-fifty we were parked—legally, for a change— about half a block from the Gresham Hotel on West Twenty-third Street. The daylight was fading fast now. Carolyn rolled down her window and snapped a quick picture of a passing stranger. The result wasn't too bad from an aesthetic standpoint, but the dim light resulted in a loss of detail.

"I was afraid of that," I told her. "I booked the Maharajah at five and Whelkin at six, and then when I spoke to Demarest, I was going to set up the call for seven. I made it four instead when I remembered we'd need light."

"There's flashcubes in the carrying case."

"They're a little obvious, don't you think? Anyway,

I'm glad we caught Demarest when it was still light enough out to see him. With Whelkin it may not matter. We may not be able to coax him out of the hotel."

"You think he's staying there?"

"It's certainly possible. I'd have called, but what name would I ask for?"

"You don't think he's staying there under his own name?"

"In the first place, no. In the second place, I have no idea what his right name might be. I'm sure it's not Rudyard Whelkin. That was a cute story, being named for Kipling and growing up to collect him, but I have the feeling I'm the only person he told it to."

"His name's not Rudyard Whelkin?"

"No. And he doesn't collect books."

"What does he do with them?"

"I think he sells them. I think"—I looked at my watch—"I think he's sitting in a booth in the lobby of the Gresham," I went on, "waiting for my call. I think I better call him."

"And I think I better take his picture."

"Be subtle about it, huh?"

"That's my trademark."

The first phone I tried was out of order. There was another one diagonally across the street but someone was using it. I wound up at a phone on the rear wall of a Blarney Rose bar that had less in common with Sangfroid than the Hotel Gresham did with the Carlyle. Hand-lettered signs over the back bar offered double shots of various brands of blended whiskey at resistibly low prices.

I dialed the number Whelkin had given me. He must have had his hand on the receiver because he had it off the hook the instant it started to ring.

The conversation was briefer than the one I'd had with the Maharajah. It took longer than it had to because I had trouble hearing at one point; the television announcer was delivering football scores and something he said touched off a loud argument that had something to do with Notre Dame. But the shouting subsided and Whelkin and I resumed our chat.

I apologized for the interference.

"It's nothing, my boy," he assured me. "Things are every bit as confused where I am. A Eurasian chap's sprawled on a bench in what looks to be a drug-induced coma, a wild-eyed old woman's pawing through a shopping bag and nattering to herself, and another much younger woman's flitting about taking everyone's picture. Oh, dear. She's headed this way."

"She sounds harmless," I said.

"One can only hope so. I shall give her a dazzling smile and let it go at that."

A few minutes later I was back in the Pontiac studying a close-up of Rudyard Whelkin. He was showing all his teeth and they fairly gleamed.

"Subtle," I told Carolyn.

"There's a time for subtlety," she said, "and there's a time for derring-do. There is a time for the rapier and a time for the bludgeon. There is a time for the end-around play and a time to plunge right up the middle."

"There's a Notre Dame fan in the Blarney Rose who would argue that last point with you. I wanted a drink by the time I got out of there. But I had the feeling they were out of Perrier."

"You want to stop someplace now?"

"No time."

"What did Whelkin say?"

I gave her the *Reader's Digest* version of our conversation as I headed uptown and east again. When I finished she frowned at me and scratched her head. "It's too damned confusing," she complained. "I can't tell who's lying and who's telling the truth."

"Just assume everybody's lying. That way the occasional surprises will be pleasant ones. I'll drop you at the Blinns' place. You know what to do?"

"Sure, but aren't you coming in?"

"No need, and too many other things to do. You know what to do after you're through with the Blinns?"

"Have a big drink."

"And after that?"

"I think so. Want to run through it all for me one more time?"

I ran through it, and we discussed a couple of points, and by then I was double-parked on East Sixty-sixth next to a Jaguar sedan with DPL plates and a shamefully dented right front fender. The Jag was parked next to a hydrant, and its owner, safe beneath the umbrella of a diplomatic immunity, didn't have to worry about either ticket or tow.

"Here we are," I said. "You've got the pictures?"

"All of them. Even Atman Singh."

"You might as well take the camera, too. No sense leaving it in the car. How about the Blinns' bracelet? Got that with you?"

She took it from her pocket, slipped it around her wrist. "I'm not nuts about jewelry," she said. "But it's pretty, isn't it? Bern, you're forgetting something. You have to come in with me now if you want to get to the Porlock apartment."

"Why would I want to get to the Porlock apartment?"

"To steal the lynx jacket."

"Why would I want to steal the lynx jacket? I'm starting to feel like half of a vaudeville act. Why would I—"

"Didn't you promise it to the cop?"

"Oh. I was wondering where all of that was coming from. No, what Ray wants for his wife is a full-length mink, and what's hanging in Madeleine Porlock's closet is a waist-length lynx jacket. Mrs. Kirschmann doesn't want to have any part of wild furs."

"Good for her. I wasn't listening too closely to your conversation, I guess. You're going to steal the mink somewhere else."

"In due time."

"I see. I heard you mention the furrier's name and that's what got me confused."

"Arvin Tannenbaum," I said.

"Right, that's it."

"Arvin Tannenbaum."

"You just said that a minute ago."

"Arvin Tannenbaum."

"Bernie? Are you all right?"

"God," I said, looking at my watch. "As if I didn't have enough things to do and enough stops to make. There's never enough time, Carolyn. Have you noticed that? There's never enough time."

"Bernie . . ."

I leaned across, opened the door on her side. "Go make nice to the Blinns," I said, "and I'll catch you later."

SEVENTEEN

I CALLED Ray Kirschmann from a sidewalk phone booth on Second Avenue. The Bulldogs had more than doubled the point spread, he informed me dolefully. "Look at the bright side," I said. "You'll get even tomorrow."

"Tomorrow I got the Giants. They never got anybody even unless he started out ahead."

"I'd love to chat," I said, "but I'm rushed. There's some things I'd like you to find out for me."

"What am I, the Answer Man? You want a lot for a coat."

"It's mink, Ray. Think what some women have to do to get one."

"Funny."

"And it's not just a coat we're talking about. You could get a nice collar to go with it."

"Think so?"

"Stranger things have happened. Got a pencil?" He went and fetched one and I told him the things I wanted him to find out. "Don't stray too far from the phone, huh, Ray? I'll get back to you."

"Great," he said. "I can hardly wait."

I got back into the car. I'd left the motor running, and now I popped the transmission in gear and continued downtown on Second Avenue. At Twenty-third Street I turned right, favored the Hotel Gresham with no more than a passing glance, turned right again at Sixth Avenue and left at Twenty-ninth Street, parking at a meter on Seventh Avenue. This time I cut the engine and retrieved my jump wire.

I was in the heart of the fur market, a few square blocks that added up to an ecologist's nightmare. Several hundred small businesses were all clustered together, sellers of hides and pelts, manufacturers of coats and jackets and bags and accessories, wholesalers and retailers and somewhere-in-betweeners, dealers in trimming and by-products and fastenings and buttons and bows. The particular place I was looking for was on the far side of the avenue a couple doors west on Twenty-ninth Street. There Arvin Tannenbaum occupied the entire third floor of a four-story loft building.

A coffee shop, closed for the weekend, took up the ground floor. To its right was a door opening onto a small hallway which led to an elevator and the fire stairs. The door was locked. The lock did not look terribly formidable.

The dog, on the other hand, did. He was a Doberman, bred to kill and trained to be good at it, and he paced the hallway like an institutionalized leopard. When I approached the door he interrupted his exercise and gave me all his attention. I put a hand on the door, just out of curiosity, and he crouched, ready to spring. I withdrew my hand, but this did not mollify him much.

I wished Carolyn were with me. She could have given the bastard a bath. Clipped his nails, too, while she was at it. Filed his teeth down a bit.

I don't screw around with guard dogs. The only way I could think to get past this particular son of a bitch was to spray poison on my arm and let him bite me. I gave him a parting smile, and he growled low in his throat, and I went over and broke into the coffee shop.

That wasn't the easiest thing in the world—they had iron gates, like the ones at Barnegat Books—but it was more in my line of work than doing a wild-animal act. The gate had a padlock, which I picked, and the door had a Yale lock, which I also picked. No alarms went off. I drew the gate shut before closing the door. Anyone who took a close look would see it was unfastened, but it looked good from a distance.

There was a door at the side of the restaurant that led to the elevator, but it unfortunately also led to the dog, which lessened its usefulness. I went back through the kitchen, opening a door at the rear which led into an airless little airshaft. By standing on a garbage can, I could just reach the bottom rung of the fire escape. I pulled myself up and started climbing.

I would have gone right up to the third floor if I hadn't noticed an unlocked window on the second floor. It was too appealing an invitation to resist. I let myself in, walked through a maze of baled hides, climbed a flight of stairs, and emerged in the establishment of Arvin Tannenbaum and Sons.

Not too many minutes later I left the way I'd come, walking down a flight, threading my way between the bales of tanned hides, clambering down the fire escape and hopping nimbly to earth from my perch on the garbage can. I stopped in the coffee-shop kitchen to help myself to a Hostess Twinkie. I can't say it was just what I wanted, but I was starving and it was better than nothing.

I didn't bother picking the lock shut after me. The springlock would have to do. But I did draw the gates shut and fasten the padlock.

Before returning to the Pontiac, I walked over to say goodbye to the dog. I waved at him and he glowered at me. From the look he gave me I could have sworn he knew what I was up to.

It was Mrs. Kirschmann who answered the phone. When I asked to speak to her husband she said "Just a minute," then yelled out his name without bothering to cover the mouthpiece. When Ray came on the line I told him my ear was ringing.

"So?"

"Your wife yelled in it."

"I can't help that, Bernie," he said. "You all right otherwise?"

"I guess so. What did you find out?"

"I got a make on the murder weapon. Porlock was shot with a Devil Dog."

"I just ate one of those."

"Huh?"

"Actually, what I ate was a Twinkie, but isn't a Devil Dog about the same thing?"

He sighed. "A Devil Dog's an automatic pistol made by Marley. Their whole line's dogs of one kind or another. The Devil Dog's a .32 automatic. The Whippet's a .25 automatic, the Mastiff's a .38 revolver, and they make a .44 Magnum that I can't remember what it's called. It oughta be something like an Irish Wolfhound or a Great Dane because of the size, but that's no kind of name for a gun."

"There's a hell of a lot of dogs in this," I said. "Did you happen to notice? Between the Junkyard Dog defense and the Marley Devil Dog and the Doberman in the hallway—"

"What Doberman in the hallway? What hallway?"

"Forget it. It's a .32 automatic?"

"Right. Registration check went nowhere. Coulda been Porlock's gun, could be the killer brought it with him."

"What did it look like?"

"The gun? I didn't see it, Bern. I made a call, I didn't go down to the property office and start eyeballin' the exhibits. I seen Devil Dogs before. It's an automatic, so it's a flat gun, not too large, takes a five-shot clip. The ones I've seen were blued steel, though you could probably get it in any kind of finish, nickel-plated or pearl grips, anything you wanted to pay for."

I closed my eyes, trying to picture the gun I'd found in my hand. Blued steel, yes. That sounded right.

"Not a big gun, Bern. Two-inch barrel. Not much of a kick when you fire it."

"Unless that's how you get your kicks."

"Huh?"

"Nothing." I frowned. It had seemed big, compared to the little nickel-plated item I'd seen in the Sikh's enormous hand.

Which reminded me.

"Francis Rockland," I said. "The cop who was wounded outside my bookshop. What gun was he shot with? Did you find that out?"

"You still say you weren't there, huh?"

"Dammit, Ray—"

"Okay, okay. Well, he wasn't shot with the Marley Devil Dog, Bern, because the killer left it on the floor of the Porlock apartment. Is that what you were gettin' at?"

"Of course not."

"Oh. You had me goin' for a minute there. Rockland was shot—well, it's hard to say what he was shot with."

"No slug recovered?"

"Right. The bullet fragmented."

"There must have been fragments to recover."

He cleared his throat. "Now I'll deny I said this," he said, "but from what I heard, and nobody exactly spelled it out for me, but puttin' two and two together—"

"Rockland shot himself."

"That's how it shapes up to me, Bern. He's a young fellow, you know, and bein' nervous and all . . ."

"How bad were his injuries?"

"Well, it seems he lost a toe. Not one of the important ones."

I thought of Parker, going around breaking important bones. Which toes, I wondered, were the important ones?

"What did you find out about Rockland?"

"Well, I asked around, Bern. The word I get is he's young all right, which we already knew, but he's also the kind of guy who can listen to reason."

"How do you translate that?"

"I translate it Money Talks."

"There's not enough money in this one to make much noise," I said. "Unless he'll operate on credit."

"You're askin' a lot, Bern. The poor kid lost a toe."

"He shot it off himself, Ray."

"A toe's a toe."

"You just said it wasn't an important one."

"Even so—"

"Would he settle for future payment if he got a piece of the bust? If he's the ambitious kid you say he is, he'd be crazy not to."

"You got a point."

I had more than a point. I had a whole bunch of things to tell him, some of which provoked argument,

some of which did not. At the end I told him to take it
easy and he told me to take care.

It sounded like good advice for both of us.

⁓⁓⁓

The owner of Milo Arms, Inc., had a commendable
sense of humor. His Yellow Pages ad showed the company trademark, the Venus de Milo's limbless torso with
a holster on her hip. Who could resist?

I make it a point to stay out of gun shops, but one
thing I've noticed is that I don't generally notice them.
They're almost invariably located one flight above street
level. I guess they're not that keen on the drop-in trade
and the impulse shoppers.

Milo Arms didn't break the rule. They had the second
floor of a weary red brick building on Canal between
Greene and Mercer. The shop on the ground floor sold
plumbing supplies and the upper floors had been carved
into residential units. I was loitering in the vestibule,
reading names on doorbells, when a young couple left
the building, the smell of an illicit herb trailing after
them. The girl giggled infectiously while her escort held
the door for me.

The gun-shop door was a solid wooden one with the
torso-cum-holster motif repeated, along with an extensive list of the death-dealing items on sale within. There
was the usual run of locks, plus a padlock on the outside.

I gave a knock and was reassured to hear neither a
human response nor the guttural greeting of an attack
dog. Just blessed silence. I got right to work.

The locks weren't much trouble. The padlock had a
combination dial that looked like an interesting chal-
lenge, and if I hadn't been out in public view and ur-

gently pressed for time, I might have sand-papered my fingertips and tried out my Jimmy Valentine impression. Instead I tried my hacksaw blade on the thing, and when that didn't work—it was a damned good lock, made of damned good steel—I took the easy way out and unscrewed the hasp from its mounting on the jamb. There's tricks to every trade, and if you just live long enough you get to use 'em all.

God, what a grim place! I was only inside for five minutes or so, but what an uncomfortable five minutes they were. All those guns, all close together like that, reeking of oil and powder and whatever else it is that makes them smell the way they do. Infernal machines, engines of death and destruction, killers' tools.

Ugh.

I locked up carefully on my way out. The last thing I wanted to do was make it easy for some maniac to rip off a wholesale lot of guns and ammo. I even took the time to remount the padlock, leaving the hasp more tightly bolted to the jamb than I'd found it.

Guns!

Busy, busy, busy.

I found Carolyn at the Poodle Factory, where she was catching up on her bookkeeping and not enjoying it much. "This is such an *unpleasant* business," she said, "that you think there'd be money in it, wouldn't you? You'd be wrong. Well, at least there's a big show coming up at the Armory."

"Does that mean business for you?"

"Sure. You can't win ribbons with a dirty dog."

"That sounds like a proverb. How were the Blinns?"

"Their usual charming selves. I pigged out on short-bread."

"Beats Twinkies and Devil Dogs. Was Gert happy to see her bracelet back?"

"Oh," she said. "Yeah, I guess so."

"You guess so?"

"We mainly concentrated on the photographs," she said, all crisp efficiency now. She spread out the four snapshots on the mottled formica counter. "Gert never saw this guy before in her life," she said, pointing. "She's sure about that. She doesn't think she saw this one, either, but she can't swear to it."

"But she recognized the other two?"

Her forefinger hovered above one of the snaps. She'd been nibbling the nail again, I noticed. "This dude," she said, "has been around a lot. No idea when she first saw him but it was a while ago. He's been there with Madeleine and he's also been there alone, entering or leaving the building by himself."

"Fascinating. What about our other friend?"

"Artie thinks he saw them together once. And Gert says he's got a familiar look about him."

"I'll borrow this one," I said, picking one up. "See you when I see you."

✌︎❧✌︎

The Gresham's lobby had changed some since Rudyard Whelkin had described it to me over the phone. Carolyn was gone and so was the shopping-bag lady. There was a junkie nodding on a bench, but he didn't look Eurasian to me. Perhaps he'd taken over when the Eurasian went off duty.

The phone Whelkin had used was in use now. An

immense woman was talking on it. Too large for the booth, she was standing outside it and bellowing into the mouthpiece, telling someone that she had paid back the money, that she didn't owe nothing to nobody. Her presumptive creditor was evidently hard to convince.

The little man behind the desk possessed a skin the sun had never seen. He had tiny blue eyes and a small and virtually lipless mouth. I showed him the picture I'd taken from Carolyn. He gave it a long and thoughtful look, and then he gave that same long and thoughtful look to me.

"So?" he said.

"Is he in?"

"No."

"When did he leave?"

"Who remembers?"

"I'd like to leave him a message."

He handed me a pad. I had my own pen. I wrote *Please call as soon as possible* and signed it *R. Whelkin*, not to be cute but because it was the only name I could think of other than my own. A cinch he wasn't using it here, anyway.

I folded the slip, passed it to the clerk. He took it and gazed blankly at me. Neither of us moved. Behind me, the immense woman was announcing that she didn't have to take that kind of language from nobody.

"You'll want to put the message in his box," I said.

"In a while."

Now, I thought. So I can see what room he's in.

"I better do it soon," he went on, "before I forget who the message is for. You didn't put his name on it, did you?"

"No."

"Come to think of it, who *is* it for?"

"You got no call to call me that," the large woman said firmly. "A name like that, I wouldn't call a dog by a name like that. You watch what you call me."

The desk clerk had wispy eyebrows. I don't suppose they'd have been equal to their God-given task of keeping perspiration from dripping into his eyes, but it probably didn't matter because he probably avoided ever working up a sweat. He had enough eyebrows to raise, though, and he raised them now. Eloquently.

I put a twenty-dollar bill on the counter. He gave me a key to Room 311. Fifteen minutes later, on my way out, I gave it back to him.

The large woman was still on the phone. "Talk about a snotass," she was saying, "I'll tell you who's a snotass. You're a snotass, if you want my opinion."

෪ﭢ෪

Back in the Pontiac, back downtown again. God, was there no end to this? Back and forth, to and fro, hither and yon, pillar to post. Interminable.

The lot on Nassau Street was still unattended. A sign informed me it was illegal to leave a car there under such circumstances. It was not an illegality I could take too seriously at the moment. Violators, the sign assured me, would be towed at the owner's expense. It was a risk I was prepared to run.

I found a phone, dialed WOrth 4-1114. I didn't expect anyone to answer and nobody did.

I walked down to Pine Street and east to the building Prescott Demarest had emerged from hours earlier. (Hours? Weeks of subjective time.) Now only half as many windows showed lights as had done so earlier. I wished for a clipboard or a briefcase, something to make me look as though I belonged.

The lobby attendant was dozing over a newspaper but he snapped into consciousness as I entered the building. He was an older man with a tired face, probably eking out a pension. I walked toward him, then halted in mid-stride and let myself be overcome by a coughing fit. While it subsided I checked the building directory on the wall and picked out a likely firm for myself.

"Bless you," the old man said.

"Thanks."

"You want to watch that cough."

"It's the weather. Nice one day and nasty the next."

He gave me a knowing nod. "It didn't used to be like this," he said. "Weather was always something you could count on, and now everything's changed."

I signed in. *Name—Peter Johnson. Firm—Wickwire and McNally. Floor—17.* At least I wasn't calling myself Whelkin for lack of imagination. And Peter Johnson was nicely anonymous. If Wickwire and McNally was a sizable firm, they very likely had a Peter Johnson in their employ. Or a John Peterson, or something close.

I rode the elevator to the seventeenth floor. Not that he would have been likely to check the indicator, but why be sloppy? I scooted down three flights of stairs and searched the corridors until I found a door with Tontine Trading Corp. painted on its frosted glass. The office within was completely dark, as were all the other offices I'd passed. Saturday night is the loneliest night in the week, let me tell you.

It's also the longest and I had places to go and people to see. I put my ear to the glass, rapped smartly on the wooden part of the door, listened carefully, then popped the lock with a strip of flexible steel in not much more time than it takes to tell about it.

Office locks are often like that, and why shouldn't they be? There's not much point in hanging a pickproof whizbang of a lock on a door with a window in it. All you get for your trouble is a lot of broken glass.

Besides, there was a man downstairs to keep people like me from walking off with the IBM Selectrics, and what else was there to steal? I certainly didn't find anything. When I left the Tontine office—and walked up to 17 and rode down from there—I didn't have anything with me that I hadn't carried into the building.

The old man looked up from his paper. "Now that was quick," he said.

"Like a bunny," I agreed, and signed myself out.

EIGHTEEN

"I suppose you're wondering why I summoned you all here."

Well, how often do you get to use a line like that? Here they all were, gathered together at Barnegat Books. When I bought the store from old Litzauer I'd had visions of little informal assemblies like this one. Sunday-afternoon poetry readings, say, with little glasses of medium-dry sherry and a tray of cucumber sandwiches handed round. Literary kaffee klatsches, with everybody smoking European cigarettes and arguing about what Ionesco really meant. I figured it would bring people around and garner the shop some useful word-of-mouth publicity. More to the point, it sounded like a great way to meet girls.

This evening's convocation was not quite what I'd had in mind. No one was snarling in iambs or trochees. Kafka's name had not come up. The store had already had more publicity than it needed. And I didn't expect to meet any girls.

The only one on hand, Carolyn, was perched on the high stool I used for fetching the loftier volumes from the loftier shelves. She sat off to one side, while the rest of my guests were strung out in an irregular half-circle facing the sales counter. I myself was standing behind the counter; I didn't have a chair to sit on because the one I usually kept behind the counter was occupied at the moment by Prescott Demarest.

See, my place was a bookstore, not a library. There weren't enough chairs to go around. The Maharajah of Ranchipur had the best seat in the house, a swivel-based oak armchair from my office in back. Atman Singh, his spine like a ramrod, sat upon an upended wooden packing case that had held Rome Beauty apples sometime in the dim past before Mr. Litzauer used it to store surplus stock. Rudyard Whelkin had a folding chair Carolyn had brought over from the Poodle Factory.

I hadn't introduced anyone to anyone else, nor had any of them seen fit to offer small talk about football or the weather or crime in the streets. They'd arrived not in a body but all within a fairly brief span of time, and they'd remained remarkably silent until I did my suppose-you're-wondering number. Even then, all I got was a bunch of sharp stares.

"Actually," I went on, "you all know why I summoned you here. Otherwise you wouldn't have come. We're here to discuss a book and a murder."

A hush didn't fall over the room. You can't have everything.

"The murder," I went on, "was that of Madeleine Porlock. She was shot the day before yesterday in her apartment on East Sixty-sixth Street. The killer shot her once in the forehead, using a .32-caliber automatic pistol. The gun was a Marley Devil Dog, and the killer left it at the scene of the crime. He also left me at the scene of the crime, unconscious, with the murder gun in my hand."

The Maharajah frowned in thought. "You are saying you did not kill the woman."

"I am indeed. I was there to deliver a book. I was

supposed to get paid for the book. Instead I got drugged and framed, drugged by Miss Porlock and framed by the man who killed her. But"—I smiled brightly—"I still have the book."

I also had their attention. While they watched, silent as stones, I reached under the counter and came up with *The Deliverance of Fort Bucklow*. I flipped it open at random and read:

> *"Old Eisenberg was a crafty cod*
> *With the cunning of his breed,*
> *And he ate a piece of honey cake*
> *And he drank a glass of mead,*
> *And he wiped his lips and his fingertips*
> *While he swore a solemn oath*
> *That if they should go by Fort Bucklow*
> *They'd perish—not one but both."*

I closed the book. "Horrid last line," I said. "Bad verse is when you can tell which line is there to rhyme with the other, and the whole book's like that. But it didn't become the object of our attention because of its literary merits. It's unique, you see. One of a kind. A pearl beyond price, a published work of Kipling's of which only one copy exists. And this is it, right here."

I set the book on the counter. "At the time I agreed to steal this book," I went on, "it was in the personal library of a gentleman named Jesse Arkwright. I was reliably informed that he had acquired it by private negotiation with the heirs of Lord Ponsonby, who withdrew it from a scheduled auction and sold it to him." I fixed my gaze on Rudyard Whelkin. "There may have been a Lord Ponsonby," I said. "There may still be a Lord Ponsonby.

But that is not how Jesse Arkwright got his copy of *The Deliverance of Fort Bucklow."*

Demarest asked how he'd got it.

"He bought it," I said, "from the very man who engaged me to steal it back. The arrangements for the original sale were worked out by Madeleine Porlock."

The Maharajah wanted to know how she came into it.

"She was Arkwright's mistress," I told him. "She was also a lifelong acquaintance of my client, who told her that he'd come into possession of an exceedingly desirable book. She in turn remarked that a friend of hers— one might almost say *client*—was a passionate collector with an enthusiasm for books. It only remained to bring buyer and seller together."

"And the sale went through?" Demarest seemed puzzled. "Then why would the seller want to steal the book back? Just because of its value?"

"No," I said. "Because of its lack of value."

"Then it is counterfeit," said the Maharajah.

"No. It's quite genuine."

"Then . . ."

"I wondered about that," I said. "I tried to figure out a way that the book could be a phony. It could be done, of course. First you'd have to find someone to write thirty-two hundred lines of doggerel in a fair approximation of Kipling's style. Then you'd have to find a printer to handset the thing, and he'd need a stock of fifty-year-old paper to run it off on. Maybe you could use fresh stock and fake it, but"—I tapped the book—"that wasn't done here. I handle books every day and I know old paper. It looks and feels and smells different.

"But even if you had the paper, and if you could print the thing and have it bound and then distress it in a subtle fashion so that it looked well preserved, how could you come out ahead on the deal? Maybe, if you found the absolutely right buyer, you could get a five-figure price for it. But you'd have about that much invested in the book by then, so where's your profit?"

"If the book is genuine," the Maharajah said, "how can it be worthless?"

"It's not literally worthless. The day after I stole it, a gentleman tried to take it from me at gunpoint. As luck would have it"—I smiled benignly at Atman Singh—"he selected the wrong book by mistake. But he tried to placate me by giving me five hundred dollars, and coincidentally enough, that's a fair approximation of the book's true value. It might even be worth a thousand to the right buyer and after the right sort of build-up, but it's certainly not worth more than that."

"Hey, c'mon, Bern." It was Carolyn piping up from the crow's nest. "I feel like I missed a few frames, and I was around for most of it. If it's supposed to be worth a fortune, and it's not a phony, why's it only worth five hundred or a thousand?"

"Because it's genuine," I said. "But it's not unique. Kipling had the book privately printed in 1923 in a small edition. That much was true. What wasn't true was the appealing story about his incinerating every copy but one. There are quite a few copies in existence."

"Interesting thought," Prescott Demarest said. He was dressed as he'd been when Carolyn took his picture, but then I'd simply been able to see that he was wearing a dark suit. Now I could see that it was navy blue, with a muted stripe that had been invisible in the photograph. He straightened in my chair now. "So the book's one of many," he said. "How do you know that, Rhodenbarr?"

"How did I find it out?" It wasn't quite the question

he'd asked but it was one I felt like answering. "I stole a copy from Jesse Arkwright's house Wednesday night. Thursday I delivered that copy to Madeleine Porlock's apartment. I was drugged and the book was gone when I came to. Then last night I returned to the Porlock apartment"—gratifying, the way their eyes widened—"and found *The Deliverance of Fort Bucklow* in a shoe box in the closet.

"But it wasn't the same copy. I figured it was possible that she could have stowed the book in the closet before admitting her killer to the apartment. But wouldn't he look for the book before he left? Wouldn't he have held the gun on her and made her deliver it before shooting her? He'd taken the trouble to scoop up five hundred dollars of my money before he left. Either he or Porlock took the money out of my back pocket, and if she took it, then he must have taken it from her himself, because it wasn't there to be found." The cops could have taken it, I thought, but why muddy the waters by suggesting that possibility?

"My copy was all neatly wrapped in brown paper," I went on. "Now Madeleine Porlock might have unwrapped it before she hid it, just to make sure it wasn't a reprint copy of *Soldiers Three* or something equally tacky." I avoided Atman Singh's eyes. "If so, what happened to the brown paper? I didn't see it on the floor when I came to. Granted, I might not have noticed it or much else under the circumstances, but I looked carefully for that paper when I tossed the apartment last night, and it just plain wasn't there. The killer wouldn't have taken it and the police would have had no reason to disturb it, so what happened to it? Well, the answer's clear enough now. It was still fastened around the book when the killer walked off with it. Madeleine Porlock most likely had the wrapped book in her hands when he shot her, and he took it as is."

"That's quite a conclusion," Rudyard Whelkin said. "My boy, it would seem that your only clues were clues of omission. Rather like the dog that didn't bark, eh? Five hundred missing dollars, a missing piece of brown paper. Rather thin ice, wouldn't you say?"

"There's something else."

"Oh?"

I nodded. "It's nothing you could call evidence. Pure subjective judgment. I sat up reading that book Wednesday night. I held it in my hands, I turned the pages. Last night I had my hands on it again and it wasn't the same book. It was inscribed to H. Rider Haggard, same as the copy I stole from Arkwright, but there was something different about it. I once knew a man with a yard full of laying hens. He swore he could tell those birds apart. Well, I can tell books apart. Maybe one had some pages dog-eared or a differently shaped water stain—God knows what. They were different books. And, once I realized that, I had a chance to make sense of the whole business."

"How?"

"Let's say, just hypothetically, that someone turned up a carton of four or five dozen books in the storage room of a shuttered printshop in Tunbridge Wells." I glanced at Whelkin. "Does that sound like a reasonable estimate?"

"It's your hypothesis, my boy."

"Call it fifty copies. The entire edition, or all that remains of it, outside of the legendary long-lost copy the author was supposed to have presented to H. Rider Haggard. Now what would those books bring on the market? A few hundred dollars apiece. They'd be legitimate rarities, and Kipling's becoming something of a hot ticket again, but this particular work is not only a minor effort but distinctly inferior in the bargain. It has curiosity value rather than literary value. The books would still be worth hauling home from the printshop, but suppose they could be hawked one at a time as unique specimens? Suppose each one were furnished with a forged inscription in a fair approximation of Kipling's handwriting? It's hard to produce a new book and make it look old, but it's not too tricky to scribble a new inscription in an old book. I'm sure there are ways to treat ink so that it looks fifty years old, with that iridescence some old inscriptions have.

"So my client did this. He autographed the books or had some artful forger do it for him, and then he began testing the waters, contacting important collectors, perhaps representing the book as stolen merchandise so the purchaser would keep his acquisition to himself. Because the minute anyone called a press conference or presented the book to a university library, the game was up. All the collectors he'd stung along the way would be screaming for their money back."

"They couldn't do anything about it, could they?" Carolyn wanted to know. "If he was a shady operator, they couldn't exactly sue him."

"True, but there's more than one way to skin a cat." She made a face and I regretted the choice of words. "At any rate," I went on, "the inflated market for the remaining books would collapse in a flash. Instead of realizing several thousand dollars a copy, he'd have a trunkful of books he couldn't give away. The high price absolutely depended on the books being one of a kind. When they were no longer unique, and when the holograph inscriptions proved to be forgeries, my client

would have to find a new way to make a dishonest living."

"He could always become a burglar," the Maharajah
suggested, smiling gently.

I shook my head. "No. That's the one thing he damn
well knew he couldn't do, because when he needed a
burglar he came to this very shop and hired one. He
found out, undoubtedly through Madeleine Porlock, that
Arkwright was planning to go public with his copy of
Fort Bucklow. Maybe *public's* the wrong word. Arkwright wasn't about to ring up the *Times* and tell them
what he had. But Arkwright was a businessman at least
as much as he was a collector, and there was someone he
was trying to do business with who had more of a genuine interest in Fort Bucklow than Arkwright himself,
who had no special interest in Kipling or India or anti-
Semitic literature or whatever this particular book
might represent."

Whelkin asked if I had someone specific in mind.

"A foreigner," I said. "Because Arkwright was engaged in international commerce. A man with the
wealth and power of an Indian prince."

The Maharajah's jaw stiffened. Atman Singh inclined
his body a few degrees forward, prepared to leap to his
master's defense.

"Or an Arab oil sheikh," I continued. "There's a man
named Najd al-Quhaddar who comes to mind. He lives
in one of the Trucial States, I forget which one, and he
pretty much owns the place. There was a piece about
him not long ago in *Contemporary Bibliophile*. He's supposed to have the best personal library east of Suez."

"I know him," the Maharajah said. "Perhaps the best
library in the Middle East, although there is a gentleman
in Alexandria who would almost certainly wish to dis-

pute that assertion." He smiled politely. "But surely not the best library east of Suez. There is at least one library on the Indian subcontinent which puts the Sheikh's holdings to shame."

Mother taught me never to argue with Maharajahs, so I nodded politely and went on. "Arkwright had a brilliant idea," I told them. "He was trying to rig a deal with the Sheikh. Work up some sort of trade agreements, something like that. *The Deliverance of Fort Bucklow* would be a perfect sweetener. Najd al-Quhaddar is a heavy supporter of the Palestinian terrorist organizations, a position that's not exactly unheard of among the oil sheikhs, and here's a unique specimen of anti-Semitic literature with a whole legend to go with it, establishing a great English writer as an enemy of world Jewry.

"There was only one problem. My client had already sold a book to the Sheikh."

I looked at Whelkin. His expression was hard to read.

"I didn't read this in *Contemporary Bibliophile*," I went on. "The Sheikh was told when he bought the book that he had to keep it to himself, that it was stolen goods with no legitimate provenance. That was fine with him. There are collectors who find hot merchandise especially desirable. They get a kick out of the cloak-and-dagger aspects—and of course they figure they're getting a bargain.

"If Arkwright showed his copy to Najd, the game was up and the fat was in the fire. First off, Arkwright would know he'd been screwed. More important, Najd would know—and Arab oil sheikhs can get all sorts of revenge without troubling to call an attorney. In some of those countries they still chop hands off pickpockets. Imagine what they'd come up with if they had a personal grudge against you."

I stopped for breath. "My client had another reason to keep Arkwright from adding to the Sheikh's library. He was negotiating another sale to Najd, and it was designed to net him a fortune. The last thing he wanted was for Arkwright to queer it."

Carolyn said, "I'm lost, Bern. What was he going to sell him?"

"*The Deliverance of Fort Bucklow.*"

"I thought he already did."

"He sold him the Rider Haggard copy. Now he was going to sell him something a little special." I tapped the book on the counter. "He was going to offer him this copy," I said.

"Wait one moment," Prescott Demarest said. "You have me utterly confused. That copy in front of you—it's not the one you took from this man Arkwright's home?"

"No. That copy left Madeleine Porlock's apartment in the possession of the man who killed her."

"Then the book in front of you is another copy which you found in her closet?"

I shook my head. "I'm afraid not," I said ruefully. "You see, the copy from the shoe box in the closet was a second Rider Haggard copy, and how could my client possibly sell it to the Sheikh? He'd already done that once. No, this is a third copy, curiously enough, and I have to apologize for lying earlier when I told you this was the Porlock copy. Well, see, maybe I can just clear up the confusion by reading you the inscription on the flyleaf."

I opened the book, cleared my throat. God knows I had their attention now.

" 'For Herr Adolf Hitler,' " I read, " 'whose recognition of the twin Damocletian swords of Mosaic Bolshevism and Hebraic International Finance have ignited a new torch in Germany which, with the Grace of God, will one day brighten all the globe. May your present trials prove no more than the anvil upon which the blade of Deliverance may be forged. With abiding good wishes and respect, Rudyard Kipling, Bateman's, Burwash, Sussex, U.K., 1 April 1924.' "

I closed the book. "The date's significant," I said. "I was looking at John Toland's biography of Hitler before you gentlemen arrived. One of the fringe benefits of owning a bookstore. The date Kipling supposedly inscribed this book was the very day Hitler was sentenced to five years in Landsberg Prison for his role in the Munich Beer Hall Putsch. A matter of hours after the sentence was announced he was in his cell writing the title page of *Mein Kampf*. Meanwhile, Rudyard Kipling, moved by the future Führer's plight, was inscribing a book to him. There's some rubber stamping in ink on the inside front cover, too. It's in German, but it seems to indicate that the book was admitted to Landsberg Prison in May of 1924. Then there are some marginal notes here and there, presumably in Hitler's hand, and some underlining, and some German phrases scribbled on the inside back cover and the blank pages at the back of the book."

"Hitler might have had it in his cell with him," Rudyard Whelkin said dreamily. "Took inspiration from it. Tried out ideas for *Mein Kampf*—that's what those scribbles could indicate."

"And then what happened to the book?"

"Why, that's still a bit vague. Perhaps the Führer presented it to Unity Mitford and it found its way back to Britain with her. That's not an unappealing little story. But all the details have yet to be worked out."

"And the price?"

Whelkin raised his imposing eyebrows. "For Adolf Hitler's personal copy of a work of which only one other copy exists? For a source book for *Mein Kampf*? Inscribed to Hitler and chock-full of his own invaluable notes and comments?"

"How much money?"

"Money," Whelkin said. "What is money to someone like Najd al-Quhaddar? It flows in as fast as the oil flows out, more money than one knows what to do with. Fifty thousand dollars? One hundred thousand? A quarter of a million? I was just beginning to dangle the bait, you see. Just letting that Arab get the merest idea of what I had to offer. The ultimate negotiations would have to be positively Byzantine in their subtlety. How much would I have demanded? How much would he have paid? At what point would the bargain be struck?" He spread his hands. "Impossible to say, my boy. What is that phrase of Dr. Johnson's? 'Wealth beyond the dreams of avarice.' Avarice is quite a dreamer, you know, so his words might be the slightest bit hyperbolic, but suffice it to say that the book would have brought a nice price. A very nice price."

"But not if Arkwright ruined the deal."

"No," Whelkin said. "Not if Mr. Arkwright ruined the deal."

"How much did he pay you for his copy?"

"Five thousand dollars."

"And the Sheikh? He'd already bought a copy with the Haggard inscription."

He nodded. "For a few thousand. I don't remember the figure. Is it of great importance?"

"Not really. How many other copies did you sell?"

Whelkin sighed. "Three," he said. "One to a gentleman in Fort Worth who is under the impression that it was surreptitiously removed from the Ashmolean at Oxford by a greedy sub-curator with gambling debts. He'll never show it around. Another to a retired planter who lives in the West Indies now after making a packet in Malayan rubber. The third to a Rhodesian diehard who seemed more excited by the poem's political stance than its collector value. The Texan paid the highest price—eighty-five hundred dollars, I believe. I was selling off the books one by one, you see, but it was a laborious proposition. One couldn't advertise. Each sale called for extensive research and elaborate groundwork. My travel expenses were substantial. I was living reasonably well and covering my costs, but I wasn't getting ahead of the game."

"The last copy you sold was to Arkwright?"

"Yes."

"How did you know Madeleine Porlock?"

"We were friends of long standing. We'd worked together now and again, over the years."

"Setting up swindles, do you mean?"

"*Commercial enterprises* is a less loaded term, wouldn't you say?"

"How did a copy of *Fort Bucklow* get in her closet?"

"It was her commission for placing a copy with Arkwright," he said. "I needed cash. Normally I'd have given her a thousand dollars or so for arranging the sale. She was just as pleased to have the book. She expected to sell it eventually for a good sum. She knew, of course, not to do anything with it until I'd had my shot at the big money with Najd al-Quhaddar."

"Meanwhile, you needed Arkwright's copy back."

"Yes."

"And offered me fifteen thou to fetch it for you."

"Yes."

"Where was the fifteen thousand going to come from?"

He avoided my eyes. "You'd have received it eventually, my boy. I simply didn't have it at the moment, but once I was able to place the Hitler copy with the Sheikh I'd be in a position to afford generosity."

"You might have told me that in advance."

"And where would that have gotten me?"

"Nowhere," I said. "I'd have turned you down flat."

"And there you have it." He sighed, folded his hands over his abdomen. "There you have it. Ethics are so often a function of circumstance. But I'd have settled with you in due course. You have my word on that."

Well, that was comforting. I exchanged glances with Carolyn, came out from behind the counter. "The situation became complicated," I said, "because a gentleman from India happened to be in New York at the same time as all of this was going on. Some months ago he had heard rumors about the Kipling property recently acquired by a particular Arab sheikh. Now he was contacted by a woman who told him that such a book existed, that it was presently in the possession of a man named Arkwright, that it would soon be in her possession and that she could be induced to part with it for the right price.

"The woman, of course, was Madeleine Porlock. She learned somehow that the Maharajah was in town and evidently knew of his interest in Rudyard Kipling and his works. She had a copy of *The Deliverance of Fort Bucklow*, her commission for pushing a copy to Arkwright, and here was a chance to dispose of it. She offered the book to the Maharajah for—how much?"

"Ten thousand," said the Maharajah.

"A healthy price, but she was dealing with a re-

sourceful man in more ways than one. He had her
tracked down and followed. She wore a wig to disguise
herself when she came down for a close look at me.
Maybe that was so I wouldn't recognize her when she
slipped me the doped coffee. Maybe it was because she
knew she was being checked out herself. Whatever she
had in mind, it didn't work. The Maharajah's man tagged
her to this shop, and a little research turned up the fact
that the new owner of Barnegat Books had a master's
degree in breaking and entering."

I grinned. "Are you people following all this? There
are wheels within wheels. The Maharajah wasn't going
to shell out ten grand for *Fort Bucklow*, not because he'd
miss the money but for a very good reason. He knew for
a fact that the book was a fake. For one thing, he'd heard
about Najd's copy. And you had another reason, didn't
you?"

"Yes."

"Would you care to share it?"

"I own the original." He smiled, glowing with the
pride of ownership that they used to talk about in Cadil-
lac ads. "*The* genuine copy of *The Deliverance of Fort
Bucklow*, legitimately inscribed to Mr. H. Rider Haggard
and removed from his library after his death. The copy
which passed through the hands of Miss Unity Mitford
and which may indeed have been in the possession of the
Duke of Windsor. A copy, I must emphasize, which was
delivered into my hands six years ago, long before this
gentleman"—a brief nod at Whelkin—"happened on
some undestroyed printer's overstock, or whatever one
wishes to call the cache of books from the Tunbridge
Wells printshop."

"So you wanted the phony copy?"

"I wanted to discredit it. I knew it was a counterfeit

but I could not be certain in what way it had been fabricated. Was it a pure invention? Had someone happened on a manuscript and caused a spurious edition to be printed? Or was it what I now realize it to be, a genuine book with a faked inscription? I wished to determine just what it was and establish that Najd al-Quhaddar had a similarly bogus article, but I did not want to pay ten thousand dollars for the privilege, or I would be making myself the victim of a swindle."

"So you tried to eliminate the middleman. You sent your friend here"—I smiled at Atman Singh, who did not smile back—"to collect the book from me as soon as I had it. And you instructed him to give me five hundred dollars. Why?"

"To compensate you. It seemed a fair return on your labor, considering that the book itself was of no value."

"If you think that's a fair price for what I went through, you've obviously never been a burglar. How did you know I had the book?"

"Miss Porlock informed me she would have it that evening. That indicated to me that you'd already retrieved it from its owner."

Rudyard Whelkin shook his head. "Poor Maddy," he said sadly. "I told her to hold onto the book. She'd have spiked an enormous sale of mine by what she did, but I guess she was restless. Wanted to pick up a bundle and get out of town." He frowned. "But who killed her?"

"A man with a reason," I said. "A man she double-crossed."

"For God's sake," Whelkin said. "I wouldn't kill anyone. And I certainly wouldn't kill Madeleine."

"Maybe not. But you're not the only man she crossed. She did a job on everybody, when you stop to think about it. She drugged me and stole a book from me, but I certainly didn't kill her. She was fixing to swindle the Maharajah, and he might well have felt a certain resentment when his agent came back from my shop with a worthless copy of *Soldiers Three*. But this wouldn't leave him feeling betrayed because he didn't expect anything more from the woman. Neither did I. We never had any reason to trust her in the first place, so how could we feel betrayed? There's only one man she really betrayed."

"And who might that be?"

"Him," I said, and leveled a finger at Prescott Demarest.

Demarest looked bewildered. "This is insane," he said levelly. "Utterly insane."

"Why do you say that?"

"Because I've been wondering what I'm doing in this madhouse and now I find myself accused of murdering a woman I never even heard of before tonight. I came here to buy a book, Mr. Rhodenbarr. I read a newspaper advertisement and made a telephone call and came here prepared to spend substantial money to acquire an outstanding rarity. I've since heard some fascinating if hard-to-grasp story about genuine books with fake inscriptions, and some gory tales of double-crosses and swindles and murders, and now I find myself accused of homicide. I don't want to buy your book, Mr. Rhodenbarr, whether it's inscribed to Hitler or Haggard or Christ's vicar on earth. Nor do I want to listen to any further rubbish of the sort I've heard here tonight. If you'll excuse me . . ."

He started to rise from his chair. I held up a hand, not very threateningly, but it stopped him. I told him to sit down. Oddly enough, he sat.

"You're Prescott Demarest," I said.

"I thought we weren't using names here tonight. Yes, I am Prescott Demarest, but—"

"Wrong," I said. "You're Jesse Arkwright. And you're a murderer."

NINETEEN

"I watched you this afternoon," I told him. "I saw you leave an office building on Pine Street. I'd never seen you before in my life but I knew there was something familiar about you. And then it came to me. Family resemblance."

"I don't know what you're talking about."

"I'm talking about the portraits in your library in Forest Hills. The two ancestors in the oval frames whose job it is to bless the pool table. I don't know if you're really a descendant of the guy who put the Spinning Jenny together, but I'm willing to believe the codgers on the wall are legitimate forebears of yours. You look just like them, especially around the jawline."

I glanced at Whelkin. "You sold him a book," I said. "Didn't you ever meet him?"

"Maddy handled everything. She was the middleman."

"Middleperson, I think you mean. I suppose you spoke to him on the telephone?"

"Briefly. I don't recognize the voice."

"And you?" I asked the Maharajah. "You phoned Mr. Arkwright this morning, didn't you?"

"This could be the man whose voice I heard. I am unable to say one way or the other."

"This is absurd," Demarest said. Hell, let's call him Arkwright. "A presumed resemblance to a pair of portraits, an uncertain identification of a voice supposedly heard over a telephone—"

"You forget. I saw you leave an office building on Pine Street. I called you there at a certain number, and the phone you answered was in the office of Tontine Trading Corp., and the owner of Tontine is a man named Jesse Arkwright. I don't think you're going to get very far insisting the whole thing's a case of mistaken identity."

He didn't take much time to think it over. "All right," he said. "I'm Arkwright. There's no reason to continue the earlier charade. I received a call earlier today, apparently from this gentleman whom you call the Maharajah. He wanted to know if I still possessed a copy of *Fort Bucklow.*"

"I had seen the advertisement," the Maharajah put in, "and I wondered at its legitimacy. When I was unable to obtain the book either from this store or from Miss Porlock, I thought it might remain in Mr. Arkwright's possession. I called him before responding to the advertisement."

"And he referred to the ad," Arkwright went on. "I looked for myself. I called you on the spur of the moment. I thought I could poke around and find out what was going on. A book disappeared from my house in the middle of the night. I wanted to see if I could get it back. I also wanted to determine whether it was indeed the rarity I'd been led to believe it was. So I called you, and came here tonight to bid on the book if it came to that. But none of that makes me a killer."

"You were keeping Madeleine Porlock."

"Nonsense. I'd met her twice, perhaps three times. She knew of my interest in rare books and approached me out of the blue to offer me the Kipling volume."

"She was your mistress. You had a kinky sex scene going in the apartment on East Sixty-sixth Street."

"I've never even been there."

"There are neighbors who saw you there. They recognized your photograph."

"What photograph?"

I took it out and showed it to him. "They've identified you," I said. "You were seen in Porlock's company and on your own. Apparently you had a set of keys because some of the neighbors saw you coming and going, letting yourself in downstairs."

"That's circumstantial evidence, isn't it? Perhaps they saw me when I collected the book from her. Perhaps she let me in with the buzzer and they thought they saw me using a key. Memories are unreliable, aren't they?"

I let that pass. "Maybe you thought she loved you," I said. "In any event, you felt personally betrayed. I'd robbed you, but that didn't make you want to kill me. It was enough for you to get my prints on everything and leave me with a gun in my hand. But you wanted Madeleine Porlock dead. You'd trusted her and she'd cheated you."

"This is all speculation. Sheer speculation."

"How about the gun? A Marley Devil Dog, a .32 automatic."

"I understood it was unregistered."

"How did you come to understand that? It wasn't in the papers."

"Perhaps I heard it over the air."

"I don't think so. I don't think the information was released. Anyway, sometimes an unregistered gun can be traced more readily than you might think."

"Even if you could trace it to me," he said carefully,

"that wouldn't prove anything. Just that you'd stolen it when you burglarized my house."

"But it wasn't in your house. You kept it in the lower left drawer of your desk in the Tontine office downtown."

"That's absolutely untrue."

The righteous indignation was fetching. I'd seen that blued-steel automatic in the study on Copperwood Crescent. And now I was telling him it had been at his office, and it hadn't, and he was steamed.

"Of course it's true," I said. "Anybody would keep the gun and the bullets in the same place. And I have the damnedest feeling that you've got an almost full box of .32 shells in that drawer, along with a cleaning cloth and a pair of spare clips for a Marley Devil Dog."

He stared at me. "You were in my office!"

"Don't be ridiculous."

"You—you *planted* those items. You're framing me."

"And you're grabbing at straws." I sailed on. "Do you still claim you weren't keeping Madeleine Porlock? If that's so, why did you buy her a lynx jacket? It's not hard to guess why she'd want one. It's a stunning garment." *Pace*, Carolyn. "But why would you buy it for her if you were just casual acquaintances?"

"I didn't."

"I looked in your closets when I was checking out a book from your library, Mr. Arkwright. Your wife had a couple of pretty impressive furs there. They all had the same label in them. Arvin Tannenbaum."

"What does that prove?"

"There's a lynx jacket in the Porlock apartment with the same label in it."

"I repeat, what does that prove? Tannenbaum's a top furrier. Any number of persons patronize him."

"You bought that jacket for Madeleine last month. There's a record of the sale in their files with your name on it and a full description of the jacket."

"That's impossible. I never—I didn't—" He paused and regrouped, choosing his words more carefully this time around. "If I were keeping this woman, as you put it, and if I did purchase a jacket for her, I would certainly have paid cash. There would surely be no record of the transaction."

"You'd think that, wouldn't you? But I guess they know you up there, Mr. Arkwright. You must be a treasured customer or something. I could be mistaken, but I have a hunch if the police looked through Tannenbaum's files, they'd find the sales record I described. They might even find the actual bill of sale in your desk at Tontine, with your name and the notation that you'd paid cash."

"My God," he said, ashen-faced. "How did you—"

"Of course I'm just guessing."

"You framed me."

"That's not a very nice thing to say, Mr. Arkwright."

He put his hand to his chest as if in anticipation of a coronary. "All of these lies and half-truths," he said. "What do they amount to? Circumstantial evidence at best."

"Circumstantial evidence is sometimes all it takes. You were keeping Porlock and your gun killed her, and you had the strongest possible motive for her murder. What was the Watergate expression? The smoking pistol? Well, they didn't catch you with the smoking pistol in your hands because you were considerate enough to leave it in my hand, but I think the D.A.'ll have enough to make your life difficult."

"I should have killed you while I was at it," he said. Positively venomous, his voice was. He was still holding onto his chest. "I should have tucked your finger around the trigger and put the gun in your mouth and let you blow your little brains out."

"That would have been cute," I agreed. "I killed her while committing a burglary, then took my own life in a fit of remorse. I haven't had a remorse attack since the fifth grade, but who could possibly know that? How come you didn't do it that way?"

"I don't know." He looked thoughtful. "I . . . never killed anyone before. After I shot her I just wanted to get away from there. I never even thought of killing you. I simply put the gun in your hand and left."

Beautiful. A full admission, and as much as anyone was likely to get without reading him his rights and letting him call his lawyer. It was about time for the cavalry to make its appearance. I started to turn toward the rear of the store, where Ray Kirschmann and Francis Rockland were presumably taking in all of this, when the hand Arkwright had been clutching to his breast snaked inside his jacket and back out again, and when it reappeared there was a gun in it.

He pushed his chair back as he drew the gun, moving briskly backward so that he could cover the four of us at once—Whelkin and Atman Singh and the Maharajah. And me, at whom the gun was pointed. It was a larger gun than the one I'd come to clutching, far too large to be a Whippet or a Devil Dog. And a revolver, I noted. Perhaps, if he was partial to the Marley line, it was a Mastiff. Or a Rhodesian Ridgeback, or whatever.

"Let's hold it right there," he said, waving the gun around. "I'll shoot the first person who moves a hair. You're a clever man, Rhodenbarr, but it won't do you any good this time. I don't suppose the world will miss a burglar. They ought to gas people like you in the first place, loathsome vermin with no respect for property rights. As for you"—this to Whelkin—"you cheated me. You employed Madeleine to swindle me out of some money. You made a fool of me. I won't mind killing you. You other gentlemen have the misfortune of being present at an awkward time. I regret the necessity of doing this—"

Killing women's bad policy. Ignoring them can be worse. He'd forgotten all about Carolyn, and he was still running his mouth when she brained him with a bronze bust of Immanuel Kant. I'd been using it as a bookend, in the Philosophy and Religion section.

TWENTY

At a quarter to twelve Monday morning I hung the *Out to Lunch* sign in the window and locked up. I didn't bother with the iron gates, not at that hour. I went to the place Carolyn had patronized Thursday and bought felafel sandwiches and a container of hummus and some flat crackers to scoop it up with. They were oddly shaped and reminded me of drawings of amoebae in my high-school biology textbook. I started to order coffee too but they had mint tea and that sounded interesting so I picked up two containers. The counterman put everything in a bag for me. I still didn't know if he was an Arab or an Israeli, so instead of chancing a *shalom* or a *salaam* I just told him to have a nice day and let it go at that.

Carolyn was hard at work combing out a Lhasa Apso. "Thank God," she said when she saw me, and popped the fluffy little dog into a cage. "Lunchtime, Dolly Lama. I'll deal with you later. Whatcha got, Bern?"

"Felafel."

"Sensational. Grab a chair."

I did and we dug in. Between bites I told her that everything looked good. Francis Rockland wouldn't be hassling either me or the Sikh, having accepted three thousand of the Maharajah's American dollars as compensation for his erstwhile toe. It struck me as a generous settlement, especially so when you recalled that he'd shot the toe off all by his lonesome. And I gather a few more rupees found their way into Ray Kirschmann's pocket. Money generally does.

Rudyard Whelkin, who incredibly enough proved to have a walletful of identification in that unlikely name, was booked as a material witness and released in his own recognizance. "I'm pretty sure he's out of the country," I told Carolyn. "Or at least out of town. He called me last night and tried to talk me into parting with the Hitler copy of *The Deliverance of Fort Bucklow*."

"Don't tell me he wants to sell it to the Sheikh."

"I think he knows what that would get him. Flayed alive, for instance. But there are enough other weirdos who'd pay a bundle for an item like that, and Whelkin's just the man to find one of them. He may never make the big score he's trying for but he hasn't missed many meals so far in life and I don't figure he'll start now."

"Did you give him the book?"

"No way. Oh, he's got a satchel full of copies. I only took the Hitler specimen from his room at the Gresham. I left him some Haggard copies and a few that hadn't been tampered with, so he can cook up another Hitler copy if he's got the time and patience. If he forged all of that once, he can do it again. But I'm holding onto the copy I swiped from him."

"You're not going to sell it?"

I may have managed to look hurt. "Of course not," I said. "I may be a crook in my off-hours, but I'm a perfectly honest bookseller. I don't misrepresent my stock. Anyway, the book's not for sale. It's for my personal library. I don't figure to read it very often but I like the idea of having it around."

The Maharajah, I told her, was on his way to Monaco to unwind with a flutter at roulette or baccarat or whatever moved him. The whole experience, he told me, had been invigorating. I was glad he thought so.

And Jesse Arkwright, I added, was in jail. Jugged, by George, and locked up tighter than the Crown jewels. They'd booked the bastard for Murder One and you can't get bailed out of that charge. Doesn't matter how rich you are.

"Not that he'll be imprisoned on that charge," I explained. "To tell you the truth, I'll be surprised if the case ever comes to trial. The evidence is sketchy. It might be enough to convict a poor man but he's got the bread for a good enough lawyer to worm his way out. He'll probably plead to a reduced charge. Manslaughter, say, or overtime parking. He'll pull a sentence of a year or two and I'll bet you even money he won't serve a day. Suspended sentence. Wait and see."

"But he killed that woman."

"No question."

"It doesn't seem fair."

"Few things do," I said philosophically. Move over, Immanuel Kant. "At least he's not getting off scot-free. He's behind bars even as we speak, and his reputation is getting dragged through the mud, and he'll pay a lot emotionally and financially even if he doesn't wind up serving any prison time for what he did. He's lucky, no question, but he's not as he thought he'd be before you nailed him with the bookend."

"It was a lucky shot."

"It was a perfect strike from where I stood."

She grinned and scooped up some hummus. "Maybe I'm what the Mets could use," she said.

"What the Mets could use," I said, "is divine intercession. Anyway, lots of things aren't fair. The Blinns are getting away with their insurance claim, for example. I'm off the hook for burglarizing their apartment. The police agreed not to press charges in return for my cooperation in collaring Arkwright for murder, which is pretty decent of them, but the Blinns still get to collect for all the stuff I stole, which I didn't steal to begin with, and if that's fair you'll have to explain it to me."

"It may not be fair," she said, "but I'm glad anyway. I like Gert and Artie."

"So do I. They're good people. And that reminds me."

"Oh?"

"I had a call from Artie Blinn last night."

"Did you? This mint tea's terrific, incidentally. Sweet, though. Couldn't you get it without sugar?"

"That's how it comes."

"It's probably going to rot my teeth and my insides and everything. But I don't care. Do you care?"

"I can't get all worked up about it. There was something Artie wanted to know, to get back to Artie."

"There are things *I've* been wanting to know," she said. "Things I've been meaning to ask you."

"Oh?"

"About Rudyard Whelkin."

"What about him?"

"Was he really drugged when he set up the appointment with you? Or did he just sound that way?"

"He just sounded that way."

"Why? And why didn't he show up at Porlock's place?"

"Well, it was her idea. Her reason was that she was going to sandwich in a meeting with the Maharajah so she could sell him the odd copy of the book. She certainly didn't want Whelkin around while all that was going on. The way she sold it to him was leave things open so that I wouldn't know he was involved in double-crossing me. He could always get in touch with me later on and explain that he'd been doped, too, and that was why he missed the appointment. Of course, all of that went sour when Arkwright gave her a hole in the head. But that's why he sounded groggy when I spoke to him— he was putting on an act in advance."

She nodded thoughtfully. "*I* see," she said. "A subtle pattern begins to emerge."

"Now if we can get back to Artie Blinn—"

"What happened to your wallet?"

"Arkwright took it and stuck it under a cushion where the cops would be sure to find it. I told you, didn't I? That's how they knew to suspect me."

"But what happened to it since then?"

"Oh," I said. I patted my pocket. "I got it back. They had it impounded as evidence, but no one could say exactly what it was evidence of, and Ray talked to somebody and I got it back."

"What about the five hundred dollars?"

"It was either gone before the cops got it, or some cop made a profit on the day. But it's gone now." I shrugged. "Easy come, easy go."

"That's a healthy attitude."

"Uh-huh. Speaking of Artie—"

"Who was speaking of Artie?"

"Nobody was, but we're going to. Artie wanted to know what happened to the bracelet."

"Shit."

"He said he asked you about it when you were over there with the photographs, but you said you'd forgotten to bring it along."

"Double shit."

"But I seem to remember that I asked you about it

just before you got out of the car, and you said you had it right there in your pocket."

"Yeah," she said. She drank some more of the mint tea. "Well, I lied, Bernie."

"Uh-huh."

"Not to you. To Artie and Gert. It was in my pocket but I told him it wasn't."

"I'll bet you had a super reason."

"As a matter of fact I had a shitty reason. I kept thinking how nice it would look on a certain person's arm."

"The certain person wouldn't be Miranda Messinger, I don't suppose."

"It's your intuitive brilliance that makes me love you, Bernie."

"Here I thought it was my engaging smile. Does she like the bracelet?"

"Loves it." She grinned up at me. "I went over there last night to return the Polaroid. She never even noticed it was missing. I gave her the bracelet as a peace offering, and I told her everything, and—"

"And you're back together again."

"Well, last night we were. I wouldn't want to make any long-range projections. I'll tell you, the way to that woman's heart is through her wrist."

"Whatever works."

"Yeah. 'You wouldn't want to go and wear it on the East Side,' I told her. 'Because it's just the least bit hot.' "

"Did you talk like that when you told her? Out of the side of your mouth?"

"Yeah. It really got to her. I swear the next time I buy her something I'm gonna tell her I stole it." She sighed. "Okay, Bern. What do we do about the Blinns?"

"I'll think of something."

"I was gonna tell you, but—"

"I could tell you were eager to discuss it. The way you were so anxious to talk about the Blinns and all."

"Well, I—"

"It's cool," I said. "Relax and eat your hummus."

ᴗᴖᴗ

A little later she said, "Listen, Randy's got a dance class tonight. You want to come by after work? We can have dinner in or out and then catch a movie or something."

"I'd love to," I said, "but tonight's out."

"Heavy date?"

"Not exactly." I hesitated, then figured what the hell. "When we meet for drinks tonight," I said, "I'll make mine Perrier."

She sat forward, eyes wide. "No shit. You're going on a caper?"

"That's not the word I'd use, but yeah, that's about it."

"Where?"

"Forest Hills Gardens."

"The same neighborhood as the last time?"

"The same house. The coat I described to Ray Kirschmann wasn't a fantasy. I saw it Wednesday night in Elfrida Arkwright's closet. And I promised it to Ray, and when I make promises to cops I like to keep them. So I'm going back there tonight to get it."

"Won't Elfrida object?"

"Elfrida's not home. She visited her hubby in jail yesterday, and then she went home and thought things through, and then she packed a bag and took off for parts unknown. Home to Mama, maybe. Or home to Palm

Beach. I guess she didn't want to stick around for the notoriety."

"I can dig that." She cocked her head and there was a faraway look in her eye. "He's got it coming," she said. "The bastard killed his mistress and he's not going to serve time for it. I remember when you were describing the house to me, Bern. You said you wanted to back up a truck onto the front lawn and steal everything from the chandeliers down to the rugs."

"I had the impulse."

"Is that what you're gonna do?"

"No."

"You're just taking the coat?"

"Well . . ."

"You said there was jewelry, didn't you? Maybe you can find something to replace Gert Blinn's bracelet."

"The thought had crossed my mind."

"And there's a coin collection."

"I remember the coin collection, Carolyn."

"I remember the other things you mentioned. Are you going to take the Pontiac?"

"I think that might be pushing my luck."

"You'll steal some other car, then."

"I suppose so."

"Take me with you."

"Huh?"

"Why not?" She leaned forward, laid a hand on my arm. "Why the hell not, Bern? I can help. I didn't get in the way when we stole Randy's Polaroid, did I?"

"We *borrowed* Randy's Polaroid."

"Bullshit. We stole it. Then we happened to give it back when we were done with it. If you look at it that way, I'm an old hand at this breaking-and-entering business. Take me along, Bern. Please? I'll get rubber gloves and cut the palms out, I'll pass up my after-work drink, I'll do anything you say. *Please?*"

"Jesus," I said. "You're . . . you're an honest citizen, Carolyn. No record. A respectable position in the community."

"I wash dogs, Bern. Big hairy deal."

"There's a risk."

"Screw the risk."

"And I always work alone, see. I never use a partner."

"Oh." Her face fell. "Well, that's it, then. I didn't think of it that way. I'd probably be a drag anyway, wouldn't I? It's okay, Bern. I don't mind."

"No drink after work."

"Not a drop. I can come?"

"And you can't ever tell a soul. Not Randy, not some future lover. Nobody."

"My lips are sealed. Are you serious? I can come?"

I shrugged. "What the hell," I said. "You were handy the other night. You might be useful to have around."

BIBLIOGRAPHY

THE EVAN TANNER SERIES
The Thief Who Couldn't Sleep, 1966

The Canceled Czech, 1966

Tanner's Twelve Swingers, 1967

Two For Tanner, 1968

Tanner's Tiger, 1968

Here Comes A Hero, 1968

Me Tanner, You Jane, 1970

Tanner on Ice, 1998

THE CHIP HARRISON SERIES
No Score, 1970.

Chip Harrison Scores Again, 1971

Make Out With Murder, 1974

The Topless Tulip Caper, 1975

THE MATTHEW SCUDDER SERIES
The Sins of the Fathers, 1976

In the Midst of Death, 1976

Time to Murder and Create, 1977

A Stab in the Dark, 1981

Eight Million Ways to Die, 1982

When the Sacred Ginmill Closes, 1986

Out on the Cutting Edge, 1989

A Ticket to the Boneyard, 1990
A Dance at the Slaughterhouse, 1991
A Walk Among the Tombstones, 1992
The Devil Knows You're Dead, 1993
A Long Line of Dead Men, 1994
Even the Wicked, 1997
Everybody Dies, 1998

THE BERNIE RHODENBARR SERIES
Burglars Can't be Choosers, 1977
The Burglar in the Closet, 1978
The Burglar Who Liked to Quote Kipling, 1979
The Burglar Who Studied Spinoza, 1980
The Burglar Who Painted Like Mondrian, 1983
The Burglar Who Traded Ted Williams, 1994
The Burglar Who Thought He Was Bogart, 1995
The Burglar in the Library, 1997
The Burglar in the Rye, 1999

COLLECTED SHORT STORIES
Sometimes They Bite, 1983
Like a Lamb to the Slaughter, 1984
Some Days You Get the Bear, 1993

NOVELS AND OTHER FICTION
Coward's Kiss (orig. Death Pulls A Doublecross), 1961
Mona, 1961
You Could Call It Murder (orig. Markham: The Case of the Pornographic Photos), 1961
The Girl With the Long Green Heart, 1965
Deadly Honeymoon, 1967

Such Men Are Dangerous, 1969

The Specialists, 1969

After the First Death, 1969

Triumph of Evil, 1971

Not Comin' Home to You, 1974

Ariel, 1980

Random Walk, 1988

Hit Man, 1998

NONFICTION/BOOKS FOR WRITERS
Writing the Novel From Plot to Print, 1979
  (with Cheryl Morrison)

Telling Lies for Fun and Profit, 1981

Write For Your Life, 1985

Spider, Spin Me a Web, 1988